christmas
DOGS
a literary companion

christmas DOGS

a literary companion

INTRODUCTION BY LAURIEN BERENSON

Chamberlain Bros.
a member of Penguin Group (USA) Inc.
New York

CHAMBERLAIN BROS.
Published by the Penguin Group
Penguin Group (USA) Inc., 375 Hudson Street, New York, New York 10014, USA
Penguin Group (Canada), 90 Eglinton Avenue East, Suite 700, Toronto, Ontario M4P 2Y3, Canada (a division of Pearson Penguin Canada Inc.)
Penguin Books Ltd, 80 Strand, London WC2R 0RL, England
Penguin Ireland, 25 St Stephen's Green, Dublin 2, Ireland (a division of Penguin Books Ltd)
Penguin Group (Australia), 250 Camberwell Road, Camberwell, Victoria 3124, Australia (a division of Pearson Australia Group Pty Ltd)
Penguin Books India Pvt Ltd, 11 Community Centre, Panchsheel Park, New Delhi–110 017, India
Penguin Group (NZ), Cnr Airborne and Rosedale Roads, Albany, Auckland 1310, New Zealand (a division of Pearson New Zealand Ltd)
Penguin Books (South Africa) (Pty) Ltd, 24 Sturdee Avenue, Rosebank, Johannesburg 2196, South Africa

Penguin Books Ltd, Registered Offices: 80 Strand, London WC2R 0RL, England

An application has been submitted to register this book with the Library of Congress.

ISBN 1-59609-157-6

Printed in the United States of America
1 3 5 7 9 10 8 6 4 2

Book design by Melissa Gerber

While the author has made every effort to provide accurate telephone numbers and Internet addresses at the time of publication, neither the publisher nor the author assumes any responsibility for errors, or for changes that occur after publication. Further, the publisher does not have any control over and does not assume any responsibility for author or third-party websites or their content.

Though "Fleas Navidad Nibblers" and "Yappy New Year Yum Yums" were created with your dog in mind, they should not be consumed by humans with certain food allergies.

Contents

Introduction

LAURIEN BERENSON

uring a lifetime spent in the company of dogs, there are always moments that stand out: the highs, the lows . . . and the holidays. The Christmas season is a magical time of year. Beyond the celebrating and decorating and gift giving, it's an opportunity to appreciate home and family, and all the significant relationships in our lives, especially those we share with our canine friends.

I've had the good fortune to spend my time with a number of wonderful dogs; their lives have intertwined with mine and enriched every aspect of it. There have been big dogs and small ones, young dogs and old ones; and they have each in their own way done their best—and occasionally their worst—to make the Christmas holidays memorable. Of course, I can't fault them for some of their more outrageous moments. I'd like to believe that the Christmas season brings out my better qualities, but there's a distinct possibility that the opposite may be true. Please don't ask my dogs for their opinions.

Proper planning of the perfect holiday celebration always starts several months ahead and is no trifling matter. It begins with the selection of a Christmas card. There must be a picture of the family attached, and, of course, the dogs will be included.

One year we were lucky enough to have a recent litter of puppies, six adorable white miniature poodles. In an optimistic moment, we envisioned them sitting in a basket of pine boughs with floppy red bows tied around their chubby little necks. What could possibly be cuter than that?

Not being new to dog ownership, it did occur to us that our plan contained a certain degree of folly, but we blithely dismissed our reservations and carried on. Blessed with charming naiveté early on, we imagined simple problems: the puppies might be too rambunctious to sit still for the camera, or they might become tangled up in the ribbon and require rescuing. Somehow it never crossed our minds that red satin combined with puppy drool would turn little white poodles pink. Or that the color, once stained into place, would refuse to come out despite repeated, increasingly energetic, washings.

That year we sent out a generic card, purchased by the box from the Hallmark store. It had no smiling faces, and not a single happy, playful puppy in sight. Sadly, we had to content ourselves with adding a series of small, inked paw prints near the signatures.

You would think that this experience might have taught us a lesson, but no, not really. Other Christmases we've resorted to embarrassing one of the older dogs. What dog owner doesn't have a photo of a long-suffering pet (you know that look—if they were human they'd be rolling their eyes) with a pair of stuffed antlers affixed to his head or a white cotton beard hanging from his chin? Santa hats come in varying sizes to fit every breed, and a flashing Rudolph nose always adds a nice touch. One year, lacking suitable props, I simply stuck a Christmas bow to the top of one of my poodles' heads and snapped away merrily.

Long after your children have ceased to humor you, and indeed have begun to question your sanity to their friends, your dogs will continue to bear up nobly when faced with this kind of behavior. I can only surmise it's because they love you resolutely. Though love alone isn't enough to account for the enthusiasm with which dogs throw themselves into the holiday celebration. I believe they, too, adore the pomp and ceremony of Christmas. I mean really, think about it. From a dog's point of view, what's not to like?

For openers, the holiday begins when a tree is dragged into the house. The Christmas tree stand makes a handy water bowl, located for maximum accessibility right in the living room. No need for your dog to wander all the way out to the kitchen when he's lying on the couch and feels a sudden need for refreshment. All they need to do is shimmy down under the bottom branches and lap away. How convenient!

The decorating process follows. There are tangled skeins of lights that must be wrestled into submission, and shiny Christmas balls that dangle enticingly at eye level, inviting the touch of an inquisitive nose or paw. Even better, when no one is watching, figures from the Nativity scene can be stolen and buried under the couch.

But while the joys of a canine Christmas are numerous, the family's delight isn't always as extensive.

What dog owner hasn't watched in horror as a long, sturdy tail whipped a row of ornaments from the lower branches of a tree, or looked up to find their hound sporting an unexpected halo of tinsel?

And then there's the issue of Christmas stockings. I should start by saying that in my house all socks must be scrupulously accounted for at all times. Any sock left unattended is considered to be fair game. It will be spirited away, tucked into a crate or bed, and gnawed, over time, into a juicy pulp. So taking an item that could be considered a large dog toy and dangling it from the mantelpiece is just asking for trouble. Especially if you've gone to the trouble to stuff the toe with your child's favorite Christmas cookies as I had one year. While the family was dreaming of sugarplums upstairs, the dogs decided to amuse themselves with the canine piñata I had inadvertently created. I had only myself to blame for that unfortunate misunderstanding, and a stocking to salvage before the rest of the family awoke.

A similar episode occurred the year my son, then eight, went to the trouble to make a special Christmas present for me. Having resigned himself to having only canine siblings, he constructed a picture frame to hold a photograph of my favorite dog, a poodle named Dove. He decorated the edges with markers and glued Milk-Bone dog biscuits in each of the corners before wrapping it and slipping it under the tree.

Regrettably, Dove and her relatives sniffed out the present before I did. They shredded the wrapping paper and helped themselves to all the edible artwork. Alerted by the sound of rustling paper, my son rescued the frame and was able to perform some last-minute repairs. Fortunately, we tend to keep a large supply of dog biscuits in the pantry.

Some holiday misconceptions can be harder to endure than others. Like the assumption several of my male dogs have made that a Christmas tree makes a handy indoor latrine. Each seems so surprised at my displeasure the first time this occurs. They look up at me with a wounded expression in their dark eyes. *But you brought the tree in here*, they seem to be saying, *what did you think was going to happen?*

I find myself forced to admit that they have a point. Moving a piece of the outdoors into your living room does seem to defy logic—canine or human. That's one of the beauties of sharing your life with dogs: it's a continual learning process on both your parts.

As we map out our plans for a new puppy, our heads fill with all the things we're going to teach them. But as time passes, it invariably turns out that our dogs are both wiser and more level-headed than we ever expected. In the end, they often wind up educating us.

One December my husband and I made the mistake of inviting our extended family in California and Florida to come and stay for Christmas. All right, I'll admit it: when we extended the invitation we didn't expect them all to accept. Actually we didn't expect any of them to accept. But giddy with the thought of a snowy New England Christmas, envisioning a Currier and Ives tableau, not only did the relatives take us up on our offer, they procured immediate plane reservations. And so the die was cast.

Two problems became immediately apparent. First, I come from a very contentious family. And second, my husband, son, and I lived with our four dogs in a very small house. So the addition of numerous extra relatives at the holiday was not necessarily a felicitous one.

Now add in the fact that my mother-in-law is allergic to dogs. Considering that our dogs are poodles, a breed renowned for their nonallergenic properties, it was hard to be sure whether it was actually the dogs' presence she dreaded. Perhaps it was the idea, always possible in my house, that they might jump up on her pristine clothing or invite her to play by dropping a soggy tennis ball in her lap that filled her with such alarm. She called ahead and recommended that we board the dogs for the holidays. We politely declined. I began to entertain notions of spending the holiday elsewhere myself.

That year Christmas sped toward us with all the dispatch and inevitability of an oncoming train. Every morning I ran to the window and looked out, ignoring the weather forecast from the night before and hoping against hope to find the grass and trees covered with a blanket of snow. I didn't need entire drifts. Even a dusting of flakes would have helped to set the stage.

But on the day we picked our relatives up at the airport, the sky was a clear, cloudless blue and the temperatures were unseasonably balmy. The family had just arrived and already they were disappointed with what we had to offer. Even the poodles' enthusiastic greeting upon our arrival home failed to lift their spirits.

Surely, I thought, things could only improve from that dismal beginning. Unfortunately I was wrong.

It quickly became apparent that no matter how early

I rose each morning, no matter how many extra meals I prepared or outings with a holiday theme I had planned, there was simply no way to appease all the varied interests and appetites of my guests. So I redoubled my efforts and scurried around even more, adding special ornaments to an already full Christmas tree, baking homemade treats that disappeared before they'd even had time to cool, and selecting better, more perfect, presents that would surely delight their recipients when found under the tree on Christmas morning.

By the time Christmas Eve arrived, I was thoroughly frazzled. Even the poodles, normally my staunchest allies, had begun to look at me askance. They stood at a wary distance and tipped their heads to one side as they tried to fathom what sort of frenzied, heat-breathing dragon had taken over their usually mild-mannered mom.

For my part, I was wondering how the dogs could be so sanguine about the mayhem that surrounded us. After all, it wasn't as if their lives had remained unaffected. Many of their routines and everyday habits had been unceremoniously set aside to conform to the needs of our guests.

Preferred seating on the couch, always before theirs for the asking, had been abruptly declared off-limits.

Their toys, which normally littered the house, had been swept into untidy piles and banished from sight. And more than once a poodle had found its paws trod upon by humans who—unaccustomed to sharing a home with dogs—blithely assumed that they had the right of way. Yet through it all, the dogs remained happy and agreeable.

Clearly they knew something I didn't, and I wanted in.

It took several hours of careful observation, but finally their secret was revealed. It apparently hadn't occurred to the poodles that it was their duty to be responsible for *anyone's* happiness or enjoyment of the holiday, much less for these unknown interlopers who had invaded their home for Christmas.

In the finest canine tradition, they did their best to be acquiescent. But when their efforts, like mine, predictably fell short, they didn't agonize over the result. Instead, they simply withdrew to the privacy and comfort of their own crates, snoozing contentedly with door open and one ear flapped back, in case some human with more sense than those they'd recently encountered might think to offer an enticing invitation.

It was such a simple solution that I couldn't imagine why I hadn't thought of it myself. Once the dogs' behavior pointed out the error of my ways, I couldn't wait to follow their example. And what a difference it made. My blood pressure plummeted, my hair stopped sticking straight out, and the grimace that seemed to have taken permanent hold of my features finally relaxed. The hectic Christmas household began to feel like a home again.

Alas, this isn't a fairy tale, so it doesn't have a fairy-tale ending. I wish I could say that my relatives were magically transformed too, but unfortunately since they weren't paying any attention to the poodles, they never reached the same soothing conclusion that I had. The only thing that changed really was that I discovered my family was just as happy squabbling among themselves as they would have been arguing with me.

So late on Christmas Eve when it finally did begin to snow, I didn't sing hallelujah, or brew a pot of hot cocoa, or offer to make the best snow angel anyone had ever seen. Instead I simply followed my dogs' example again. We stood in the silence of the dark night, noses pressed against the cool window, and watched the flakes swirl and eddy outside as they fell from the sky. It was the best kind of holiday moment, both serene and satisfying.

It's no wonder dogs are always included in the Nativity

scene. As a child I thought they were there to attend the shepherd, but now I know there's a bigger reason. Peace on earth and goodwill toward men is their mantra.

That's the gift that dogs offer to all those who share their space, and it's one of the reasons that the bond that formed eons ago between humans and canines continues to remain so gratifying and so strong. A paw laid gently across a knee, a look of understanding shared between old friends, the knowledge that the two of you will always be there for each other, these are the moments that make the more expansive holiday celebrations seem even more meaningful.

Christmas is many things: a time for gathering with family and friends, a reminder to think of those less fortunate than ourselves, an opportunity to make children smile with wonder and delight. Those of us who are lucky enough to spend our lives in the company of dogs know that their presence enriches almost every aspect of the holiday season. A series of wonderful writers have come together in this collection of essays to celebrate the human-canine bond. Each of them has shared Christmases with wonderful dogs and each has a story to tell of how their canine companions made a difference in their lives and in the way they experienced this special holiday.

Some of the selections are humorous, others will bring you to tears. All will engage your heart and brighten your holiday mood. You will read about adopted dogs that finally found their way to just the right home; pet lovers who pulled together to help a dog that required special care; and childhood pets that left a lasting impression on the children they loved. You'll read about dogs in need and about dogs that gave back to their communities when something was needed from them.

These are essays about people who opened their hearts and their homes for the holidays; people whose lives became inextricably bound up with dogs and who, in return, found their lives changed forever. You will find delight in tales of Tricki Woo, the overindulged Pekingese; TwylaRose, the haughty greyhound; and Dax, the empathetic Australian shepherd. There are stories, a poem, and even recipes; in short, everything you might need to celebrate the holiday with a beloved canine friend.

Best of all this book is simply filled with dogs. They come in every shape and size, and dozens of different breeds and mixes. Read on and revel in their infinite variety and their unerring natural wisdom. These are dogs at their very best. Unconcerned about what you have, they only care about who you are. And for the smallest investment of time and effort and love on your part, you will mean the entire world to them.

So turn on the Christmas lights, find an easy chair next to the fire, pour yourself a glass of eggnog, and prepare to have a good time. And while you're at it, pull a dog or two up into your lap to share the reading pleasure with you. I'm betting they'll enjoy the experience just as much as you will.

Christmas with TwylaRose
from *Chicken Soup for the Soul Celebrates Dogs*

EMMA MELLON

When I adopted TwylaRose, a retired racing greyhound, I promised myself I would treat her like a dog and not like a four-legged imitation human. She was my first dog and I had my standards. There'd be no dressing up in human clothes, no Christmas photographs with Santa, no joint shopping trips, no jewelry and no baby talk. I resolved to preserve her dogness and my dignity.

Those high sentiments crashed, one by one, beginning with the restrictions against baby talk. Though I didn't actually make goo-goo sounds on the way home from the kennel, I brimmed over with pet names: Pumpkin, Sweetie, Girlfriend, Honeybunch, Boo. . . . I hadn't expected to feel so much or to feel it so quickly.

The skinny anxious creature in the backseat spoke directly to my heart. Our first hour together transformed me into her friend and protector, parent and pal, teacher and student, sister and most dedicated fan.

As our first Halloween approached, a friend bought a top hat and tails costume for her own dog. Theoretically, I couldn't have been more opposed to the idea but it got me thinking. I enjoy Halloween and it didn't seem right to leave TwylaRose out of the festivities.

Since she came from the long line of hounds that lived as royalty with the pharaohs, I dressed her as Anubis, the deity in Egyptian mythology whose task it was to lead the deceased into the other world. Anubis appears in tomb paintings as a half-human, half-greyhound figure that weighs the human heart against its own truth in the form of a feather.

Being helped through that final passage by a god with the canine qualities of faithfulness and surefooted instinct appealed to me. I assured myself that TwylaRose as Anubis was not only a species-appropriate character, but one that was inspirational and educational as well.

I sewed a golden-brown sequined bodysuit and a small matching bag to hold the feather. Of course no one had a clue about who she was supposed to be. Even when I explained, no one much cared and TwylaRose seemed indifferent, but I enjoyed recounting the mythology and I loved the flash of sunlight off those sequins.

During that first year, I had become friends with three women who also had adopted retired racers. Our four greys became The Pack: TwylaRose, Ike, Pepper and Christa. With humans in tow, they met several times a week.

Nothing pleased the greyhounds so much as being together. They sniffed butts, stood flank to flank in greeting and draped their long necks over each other. When it was too hot or too cold to walk, we met at someone's home where the greys vied for squeaky toys or came to us for stroking, then settled into naps. Doggy play dates became part of my reality and an extended human/canine family formed.

When Christmas approached, somebody suggested we have The Pack's picture taken with Santa Claus. My early resolutions echoed against the idea but I felt the tug: Wouldn't it be sweet? Wouldn't it be fun? Wouldn't it be nice to have a picture of The Pack?

I cast around for an excuse to break my own rule. *Since I am no fan of Christmas excesses,* I reasoned, *the photo could be my*

Wegman-like comment on the season. Everyone else wants to go and it would be rude of me to resist. I said I'd do it for the good of the group. Of course, I lied. Deep down, I wanted to immortalize our Pack. I wanted to include them in our celebration of winter, like the family members they were. So I went along. I even tied a wide ribbon around TwylaRose's neck and stiffened it with a shot of spray starch.

And so we found ourselves at PetSmart one Saturday morning just before Christmas. A large pet supply chain store, PetSmart welcomes dogs to shop along with their humans. It hosts events like meets-and-greets during which various rescue groups show their dogs and take applications for adoption. In December, they host Santa.

The store was rich with the scents of dogs as well as the subtle perfume of live snakes, kittens, iguana, parakeets and parrots. It was a huge cavernous place with fluorescent light pouring down on a crowd of shoppers and their sniffing animal companions, frantic from overstimulation. Exotic birds, parrots and canaries layered the air with their cries and Burl Ives tied it all up in a fat red ribbon with his hearty and optimistic rendition of "Jingle Bell Rock."

Just inside the door, Ike began trembling so hard his

tags rattled. Pepper and TwylaRose lunged in opposite directions, and Christa hid her tail and froze. We had arrived early to avoid the crowd. Santa's white plastic bench waited at the center of the store. We stood second in line. Christa eyed the chihuahua ahead of us, her predator instinct stirring. Pepper's anxiety turned to gas, heralding intestinal distress. By now, Ike was vibrating and TwylaRose had lowered her head and was pulling toward the door.

Santa slunk in from a back room. He was human, small, and shapeless. He didn't look like the Santa in the Macy's Thanksgiving Day Parade. His shoulders rounded and his face hung expressionless until it disappeared into a tired, synthetic beard.

I felt empathy for Santa. I wouldn't want to spend my Saturday posing with overwrought dogs and trying to please their doting owners. Our Santa coped by exhibiting an indifference of mythic proportions. He sat down. The feisty chihuahua sprinted toward him and spun at his feet. Santa stared straight ahead. The human scooped up her darling and plopped him onto Santa's lap. She crouched just outside of camera range and cheered her pup on. The Polaroid flashed and it was our turn.

Trembling, farting, panting, scanning the environment for danger, tongues hanging out, ears up to monitor sounds, the greys approached for the group picture.

Santa sat there limp while we arranged the greyhounds around him, TwylaRose beside him on the bench and Christa up on the other side. TwylaRose jumped down and I lifted her up again. We draped Santa's arms over each of the girls and wrapped the fingers of his gloved hands around their collars. We arranged Ike to the right of his knees and Pepper to the left. We backed out of camera sight, holding our collective breath. Pepper broke for the door. We set him back into place.

One camera flash and it was done. We each have a copy. There is Pepper looking for the exit, Ike with his long, long tongue panting into the camera, TwylaRose whose red bow had slipped down her neck and Christa smiling at the lens.

I still believe TwylaRose deserves respect for who she is. There are still no dog pajamas in the house, though on cold nights I do throw a light blanket over her. I shop alone at the pet store. The baby talk comes and goes and mixes with adult conversations. Every Christmas I bring out the picture of The Pack with Santa. I'm learning about what it is to be a greyhound, racing and retired. And she participates when I involve us in human adventures. I may have trashed my standards but I've come to understand that tasting each other's lives is the point, and love, not foolishness, enables that to happen.

The Good Shepherd

SUSAN CHERNAK MCELROY

Tonight on the living room floor, I lined up the three green plastic Christmas tubs that live in my garage for eleven months of the year. With my back turned to the fire from the old propane heating stove, I put aside the lids and started my ritual sifting-through of the Christmas stuff. At the bottom of the third tub, I found what I was looking for: the large, ornate, tacky tree ornament made by my mother's long-passed-away friend, Mary Alice. Carefully, I unwrapped the sliced-in-half Styrofoam ball that holds on top a plastic cabin scene with a small ceramic German shepherd glued in the center. The door of the Styrofoam cabin is outlined in red sequins stuck on with straight pins. The scene is covered with pearlescent glitter "snow" that covers the back of the dog, the roof of the cabin, and the miniature plastic pine tree that lurches off to the right.

The dog figurine, made of china, is lying down with its head up and its *front paws crossed, looking exactly like my old dog Keesha, who has been gone now longer than Mary Alice. I held the ornament in the cup of my palm, and remembered other Christmases and other shepherds who have no representation on my tree. Shepherds from before the days I began any Christmas collecting of my own . . .*

There was once a Christmas keepsake I somehow lost along the way to adulthood. It was a small plaster manger statue of a Christmas shepherd with a sheep on his shoulders, a long hooked staff in his hand, and a dog pressed to his side looking keenly up into his face. The dog looked just like Rin-Tin-Tin, with pricked ears and a pointed nose. That figurine symbolized my deepest holiday longings when I was very young. No, I had no secret desires to herd sheep. Raised in an assortment of apartments and trailer parks in my youngest years, I could have no pets of any kind, and to me, the manger scene at Christmas contained all my most precious dreams: dreams of animals, of living with them and being surrounded by their sounds and scents.

Each Christmas I would fuss very carefully with the placement of the manger animals that included three sheep, a donkey, a reclining cow, and most precious of all—the shepherd with his dog. All of the animals mesmerized me, but perhaps I understood that out of all those possible creatures, a dream dog was probably most in the realm of likelihood, considering our circumstances. Practical-minded even at the age of four, I could imagine us in a house far more easily than I could imagine us on a farm with a barn and a manger.

We set up the manger every year, just as we did a fresh floor-to-ceiling Christmas tree. That tree was a part of a host of Christmas symbols like Santa and sleds and reindeers and tons of wrapped presents. The manger was something different altogether with its hay, angels, virgin, tiny infant, critters, and three black wise men. I could never reconcile the two—Santa and the manger. I don't know as how most American children possibly could. As it turned out, dogs would reconcile it for me.

Out of their own longing to appease me as best they could, my parents for many years answered my Christmas wishes for a puppy with stuffed dog toys. One year it was a Pekingese with a little puppy at her side. Another Christmas, it was a big black poodle with movable legs. I pretended all these toys were real dogs, and I played with them and slept with them and told them secrets, just as I would have done if they were living, breathing beings.

The year I found a beautiful plush collie toy under the tree was, ironically, the year that my best friend next door got a real collie puppy. Christmas morning, I hurried over to her small pink house with the Cyclone-fenced yard to show her my new dog, and was stunned speechless when she showed me hers. Wiggling, panting, his tiny pink tongue slurping kisses, her new pup leaped into my arms, knocking aside my own new "dog." I felt the fuzzy warmth, inhaled the intoxicating smell of puppy breath, then put the pup down, grabbed up my stuffed toy, and ran home heartbroken, jealous, and sobbing. I had wanted Santa that year, and Santa was about wishes answered and the correct presents in the packages under the tree. But what I got was the manger: the mystery of life, with all its birth pains, promise, confusion, and the foreshadowing of both great hope and despair.

I was nearly eight years old by the time we moved into our first house. Lady, our first real live dog, did not come home on Christmas. We were too excited to wait that long, so my family jumped the gun. It was October, and our black-and-tan German shepherd pup was just the right color for the Halloween holiday. I remember the night I first saw her being carried into the breeder's house, a squirming ball of legs and ears. At three and a half months old, she was not exactly a tiny, fuzzy pup, but she was a real, breathing, wiggling one. I was breathless with wonder and joy when my folks let her ride home in the backseat of the car with me, entranced even when she drooled buckets on my coat sleeve and then barfed in my lap. None of my stuffed dogs had ever done that!

That night in my bed, listening to Lady whimper softly in the kitchen with her new toys and old blankets, I knew that although a carved pumpkin decorated our dining room table, it was Christmas. It was the right present in the right box. The plaster dog at the heels of the shepherd figure had come early and come to life and was bedded in our house, just about a month or so ahead of regular schedule.

Lady was unique in the dog-history of my family, because she was the only puppy who consistently did all of the things puppies are naturally supposed to do, like swallow shoes, pee on the rugs, dig craters in the yard, and appear deaf to all words that sounded like commands of some sort, except "walk." She did learn to chase a ball and even to bring it back. True to her shepherd nature, she devoted herself to us, particularly to my older brother.

She followed him with her body and her eyes, looking up at his face precisely like the plaster statue from the manger figurines. She never looked at me that way, but I forgave her for that. She was funny and tender and had come near enough to Christmas to answer all of my childhood prayers at once.

By the Christmas of her blossoming second year, Lady was precious family. She was long and lanky then, and her tongue impossibly pink and long. There were no fresh piles of dirt showing up in the yard anymore, nor wet spots on the carpet. Lady was maturing fast, and her devotion to all of us, particularly my brother, had settled around her like a mantle of majesty. On family outings, she would corral us all, casting the invisible barrier of her love and protection around us like a sacred circle. Life for her and with her was perfect, except for the limp she developed at only four months of age in her hind end. My mom called it "growing pains." I knew about those things because I had them, too.

For a special treat that winter, Mom and Dad decided we would celebrate Christmas in the mountains. We reserved a little rustic cabin that welcomed dogs. My parents put all our wrapped Christmas packages in the car, loaded us up with warm cloths and snow boots, and off we went to introduce Lady to the snow. As it turned out, there wasn't much snow that year, but that was okay, because we were able to walk clear to the American River just across the highway. Lady loved the water and the woods, and when she curled up next to us in our cabin at night, tired and a bit gimpy, she smelled like pine needles and good dirt.

I still have those memories, the ones about the river and a galloping young dog, the pea-green walls of the cabin, and my small upper bunk, but I do not revisit them often. Purposefully, I have stored them away because of what happened just after Christmas Day when my parents had gone down to the lodge to have a postholiday libation and a little private time away from my brother and me.

Older than me by six years, my brother knew best about all things, or at least it seemed that way to me then. So there was nothing to question when he let Lady outside to relieve herself. She had been gone for sometime and my brother was heading to the door to call her name at the very same instant we heard the screech of tires and the loud yelp of a dog. I was out of the bunk in an explosion of fear, at the door even as my brother turned the knob and pushed it open. The instant I had heard the dog's startled voice, I had begun chanting "Not Lady . . . not Lady . . . not Lady" over and over again, very fast. But there she was in the road, in defiance of my desperate mantra, spinning in a circle on her front legs while her back end dragged motionless.

The rest of the day went by in an ugly blur. My brother was bereft and stricken and sobbing for much of it. None of us had imagined that Lady would try to find us all and keep us together, that she would search across the highway for my mom and dad, and come within ten steps of making it back across the road to the cabin. The car that struck her never even slowed down, said a fellow from the lodge who was looking out the window and saw it happen.

I remember my parents and the lodge owners trying to find a vet in town over the holidays, and the image of my mother making a palate of blankets on the cabin floor next to Lady so she could sleep there beside her. Mom says that Lady never once shut her eyes that night, and Mom could only know that because she didn't either. The next day, we learned that Lady had a broken spine. The good news—she felt no pain. The bad news—there was nothing to be done to save her. She was euthanized that day.

My parents packed our car silently. Our opened presents made a dull mockery of the season as we put them numbly into the trunk and headed home without our dog. It was another Collie Christmas to the tenth magnitude, coming back at me with far deeper grief than a child's hard envy.

Because we fled the mountains in our sorrow earlier than scheduled, there was nothing to do but sit and grieve when we got back home. Each of Lady's toys, dishes, collars, and even her pile or two of dog poop in the backyard stabbed at our collective broken heart like ice shards. In the manger by the tree, the shepherd stood with his staff and dog, looking thoughtfully at the tiny hallowed figure the size of a thimble in the matchstick manger. I sat before the figures and cried, finding bits of comfort in the familiar smell of the old hay and green moss that lined the crèche. But no angels brought Lady back, and sacred gifts of the wise men were no consolation for what we had lost.

Three days of silent misery later, my mother came into the kitchen carrying the newspaper classified ads. Behind red, puffy lids, her eyes held a faint hope. "There is a dog here for sale." She pointed to an ad with her fingertip. "A black, female German shepherd, only eight months old. Do you think we should go see her? We can't go on like this . . ." her chin began to tremble. Numbly, we nodded. Why not? What was there to lose? We felt as though we'd already lost everything.

And that is how, a day later, Sugar came to our house, slinking past us without a glance, staring dumbly out the window in despair as her former owner-breeder left her behind. At eight months of age, she had already had four owners. Her breeding and body captivated those who were eager to enter her into shows, but her coloring—coal black without a single hair of any other color—was not favored by the judges, and she was judged out of the standard. After each failed show ring success, her new people returned her to the breeder.

"Her name is not a joke," the breeder hastily informed us. "Really, she is as sweet as sugar. She just needs some stability." Secure, well-loved child that I was, I could not imagine how it would be to have and to lose four homes in eight months, but what I could not imagine, I could feel simply sitting next to this dark, sunken shadow that peered desperately, hopelessly, out the window. For three days, I sat with her there, feeling misery leach from her to me. We called the breeder with our confusion and our helplessness. "Give her time," she said. "Just some time." We brought her food to her because she would leave her vigil only to relieve herself out in the yard for brief instants before hurrying back into the house and up onto the couch. Her tail was tucked so far beneath her legs I thought for a long time that she didn't have one. Those few days felt like a month as we all sat—dog and people— silently mirroring each other's sorrow. We had our loss to bear, just as she had hers. Bringing her home crystallized our pain for us in some strange way, and yet . . . yet, feeling our deep compassion for her grief brought us silently out of the first grave weight of our own. In the corner of the room sat the manger and the tree, both seeming a bit out of place. The tree was beginning to droop. The manger stood in stillness, in that kind of stillness that is utterly beyond words. In our own very humble and very ordinary way we were each a part of that manger scene, but not the part of the angels and the Christ child. We were hunkered over in our places playing out that part before the holy coming, when the world holds its breath and there is an air of tension and even fear in the waiting. We sat in mystery and frustration. We sat, quiet, in those moments just before the miracle and the dream.

On her fourth night with us, Sugar warily followed me to my room and settled cautiously on the floor by my bedroom door, keeping a hesitant, instinctive watch. The next morning, she abandoned her post by the window and came into the kitchen for a drink of water and a Christmas cookie. Her tail was still glued to her belly, and she didn't so much walk anywhere as slink, ghostlike. Still, there was a moment or two when she looked up into my face with an aura of ancient dignity that made me catch my breath. For in that look, I saw not only the manger figurine of the shepherd and his dog, but Lady.

At the end of the first week of the New Year, we put the holiday decorations away for another year. Mom handed me a box, and I wrapped the manger figures one by one in Kleenex. A neighbor couple sat talking with my mother as we busied ourselves. "You know," the man whispered, "That limp Lady had. It was hip dysplasia. She probably would have been crippled young. . . ." In the years to follow, that is the mantra we would tell ourselves to help us make meaning of her loss. That, and Sugar, the coal-black queen who sat quietly by my side, sniffing the tree decorations as they came down, her lips eased into a tentative smile, her eyes on my face, on my brother's face, on my parents, watching us as Lady had done, and as she would continue to watch us for the next decade, home at last.

I covered baby Jesus with Kleenex and slipped him into the box next to Mary, adding the wise men and Joseph upside down because that is the only way they fit. Christmas had come and gone and come again in the space of that week, bringing its fierce honesty into the world and into the life of my family. Our Christmas had been our own journey that was something like the exhaustion of two traveling to an unwelcoming city, to a drafty barn, the two becoming three in the anxiety of a labor-filled, steaming birth in the presence of animals and angels. Out of the mystery comes a sacred miracle: Life. And in our own family miracle, there was room for Saint Nick as well, bringing the perfect gift in the perfect box. A black and regal gift full of promise and need, bearing the gift tag "From Lady, with love."

I added the shepherd figure to the top of the family pile unwrapped, and closed the box as Sugar dabbed her tongue on my hand.

Nell's Gift

MARION S. LANE

Two hours north of New York City the traffic thinned, and in spite of the snow, I began to relax behind the wheel. Nell was fast asleep on the backseat, even though the shopping bags full of Christmas presents were crowding her on one side. In the rearview mirror I could see one loop of the goofy big red bow I'd tied to her collar. Always stoic, Nell suffered the bow as she would suffer the antlers I'd place on her head the next morning when it was time to pose for photos with my cousin's kids. The red bow looked great against Nell's sleek black coat and white chest.

The snow was falling heavily now as the elevation increased and the temperatures dropped. It was Christmas Eve: my fortieth, Nell's fourth. I hated driving in the snow, but at least I'd make the trip in daylight.

What a wuss I'd become! Living in the city for twenty years had done that. People who grew up in the snowbelt, as I had, drove snow-covered roads nonchalantly, with defiance even. They had no choice. Yet here I came with my four-cylinder Escort and a short-coated dog with a big red bow. From beyond the grave my father shook his head and frowned. "Pretty poor choices for this part of the world," I heard him say softly.

I slowed to leave the New York State Thruway at Exit 19 in the Catskill Mountains. In the toll plaza, Nell roused herself when the car came to a stop. A chunky blond woman extended a gloved hand to take my money. Nell poked her muzzle out of the window and sneezed as snowflakes went up her nose.

"She's adorable," the toll taker cooed.

"Merry Christmas," I replied, and I meant it. This woman was a local, and I felt a sense of kinship.

I turned west on State Route 28. With each passing mile, we drew closer to the hamlet where I'd grown up. My parents were in the Mount Tremper cemetery, and no one in my family lived there anymore, but I always drove past our old home on my way upstate to visit relatives.

It had stopped snowing for the time being, but

previous storms and below-freezing temperatures had left the fields and lawns blanketed in white. High snowbanks lined both sides of the road. In the backseat Nell was sleeping again, lulled by the wheels turning beneath her. All those trips around the block when she was a puppy had paid off. Okay . . . maybe I'd overdone it. But so what if I couldn't pick up the car keys without her rushing to the front door of the apartment? She traveled like a trouper, just like the training books said she would.

It was noon when I pulled onto the shoulder of the road opposite my childhood home. I stared a long time at the house, then took in the woods that began at the edge of the lawn, the maple tree that my brother had planted as a teenager, the dip at the end of the garden where Pepper rested beneath the snow. Unfamiliar cars stood in the driveway, but otherwise the place hadn't changed much in the seven years since my father died. A large wreath hung on the front door that opened onto the porch.

In my mind's eye I saw Pepper curled into a tight ball in front of that door on the porch, covered with a night's fall of fresh snow. Where he went when the wind howled out of the north and blew the snow like shards of glass across the porch floor, we never knew. Somewhere he found shelter because he invariably showed up at mealtime. Animals took care of themselves, my father said.

Lost in memories, I drifted back to the present when Nell whined gently, up on her feet and looking out the window. Unlike Nell, Pepper had been in a car only twice in his life: the day we brought him home at six weeks of age, and again when he was five or six and the town held a free but mandatory rabies clinic. Pepper had never worn a collar, had never been walked on a leash, and I remember my father manhandling him into the car to take him to the clinic. A few miles from home, Pepper received his one and only vaccination. After that experience, he gave the car a wide berth.

"We're not getting out here," I told Nell, easing the Escort back onto the road. After a minute or two, I heard her flop back down and exhale noisily. Such a good dog!

Ninety minutes later I turned right off Route 10 in Richmondville and floored the gas pedal to climb up onto Bear Gulch Road. My cousin Sandy's big farmhouse, a mile and a half up the road, was "home" now. My brother and sister, their spouses and kids, Sandy's siblings and their children, my widowed aunt—all of us gathered here now at holidays. I'd come to love "the Gulch," its steep hillsides and unpaved road.

Happy as I was to be here, I felt the old defensiveness. Surrounded by people who loved me, I was still the oddball: the only one who wasn't married, who had no children, who'd gone to live in the big bad city. My siblings, my cousins, I was sure they pitied me for having to "make do" with dogs for family. They chatted about their kids, and I talked about Nell. As my words left my mouth, they slammed against some kind of species barrier. No one said "Oh, puh-leez"; in fact, they smiled appreciatively. But I knew my family wondered—and worried—what was wrong with me.

Yet who could say why, when we'd all grown up together, it was only I who'd fully felt the icy shards of snow blowing across the porch, and made a childish vow that grew only more solemn as I matured: When I grow up . . . ? I intended to do better by animals than my family had.

As one human relationship after another fell short of expectations, I finally put all my eggs in the animal basket. A career change followed, and for six years now I'd been a pet writer and pet editor at the American Society for the Prevention of Cruelty to Animals in New York City. One of the bills that our legislative staff had drafted in Albany called for "adequate shelter for dogs kept outdoors in inclement weather." I burst into tears when it became law.

I pulled into my cousin's driveway and switched off the ignition. Nell was whining in earnest now, aware of where she was and anxious to get out of the car. Soon we were inside by the woodstove, numbed by the roaring fire and a glass of eggnog. I was the last to arrive, and I began to place my gifts with all the others under the tree. Along with the books and tapes and board games, I tucked into random places small items that were addressed "To Cousin Sandy, from Nell," and another, "To Aunt Jane, from Nell." Two years ago "Nell" had begun to send gifts to the kids in the family, and they were tickled by it. Last year the youngsters had reciprocated. There had been a chew toy from seven-year-old Noah, and a small book about dogs from his brother Adam, the intellectual nine-year-old. But they were kids! Putting out gifts from my dog to adults was asking for pity and prayers. For one panicked moment I was tempted to stuff them back into my shopping bag.

When we were kids, our parents chastised us for looking too closely at the gifts beneath the tree. "You'll spoil Christmas," they said. I didn't understand it at the time, but later I realized that they thought we could tell what the gifts were from the shape and weight of the packages. And probably we could have, but we weren't focused on that. We weren't focused at all, we were so thrilled. Yet on this night at my cousin's I found myself sneaking a peek at the nametags on the packages we'd open on Christmas morning. I saw "To Jane, from Larry," "To Floyd, from Sue," "To Mom, from Noah." Digging a little deeper, I saw a few addressed to me. I loved looking at all the tos and froms, imagining the pleasures of giving and receiving. Then suddenly I saw a tag that made my throat catch. It read, "To Little Nell, from Sandy." My hand flew to cover my mouth. It took a second to process what I'd seen, even as I pushed the package aside and pretended to look at another. My cousin had given a gift to my dog! She had a dog of her own, and several barn cats, and I knew she didn't give gifts to them. Certainly Pepper had never had a Christmas gift. Even I had not imagined such a thing. I turned away from the tree and picked up my eggnog with a shaking hand.

My parents' words came back to me. Maybe I shouldn't have looked at the tags, but doing so hadn't spoiled Christmas. That night I'd be a kid again in my bed, impatient for the night to end, cherishing every moment until morning.

Nice Doggy

SUSAN ORLEAN

The other day, my Welsh springer spaniel, Cooper, gave me a manicure. He doesn't give the world's best manicure—for that you'd have to go to that Korean joint, Nuclear Nails, or whatever it's called, on Broadway—but he really tries. He can tell whether I'm in the mood to have my cuticles cut or just pushed back, and it was actually his idea to wear a little white uniform—he can just sense that it makes me more comfortable to have a "professional" atmosphere whenever I'm getting personal services. And you know how every time you get a manicure you immediately remember something you need in your handbag? And how if you put your hand in your bag to get it you wreck your nails? Cooper knows how frustrating that is to me, so as soon as he's done with my top coat he goes over to my handbag, empties the contents, and separates everything into little piles so that I can get whatever I need without making a dent in my polish.

Look, I know he's not perfect. He ate an entire pumpkin pie at Thanksgiving while I was at a performance of *Phantom*. He engages in retributive vomiting when he's left alone for more than four hours. He can, at times, smell. But in terms of totally grokking my emotions, he is off the charts. Whenever I break up with someone, Cooper is there with the complete "Hey, girlfriend" treatment: the bottle of California champagne, the fatty snacks, the comfy sweatclothes that I hadn't dared wear while courting Mr. Wrong. He doesn't dole out all the tired lines like "You're too good for him anyway" and "You are by far the best-looking and thinnest of all of our friends"; he just gives me that look, nudges the bowl of Doritos in my direction, and by his silence implies that I don't need to do anything but have myself a big old cry.

Monkeys? Sure, they're super-cute, especially when you dress them in those frilly white bonnets and little corduroy shorts. It's nice that they can acquire a complex vocabulary of gestural signs and classify sets of objects with respect to their ordinal relationship. The opposable thumb is a big whoop. But that's the thing: they have the morphology but not the motivation. Do you remember Mr. Thumb ever zipping your dress without being begged?

Recently, I got downsized at work, and then I had to listen to my so-called friends give me their "rational" assessments of the situation—the crap about my failure to meet quarterly departmental goals, my responsibility for the mold-spore contamination in the office refrigerator, the unfortunate incident with the color copier. I guess they thought that once I saw my role in getting canned I could be more philosophical. Note to "friends": Yeah, like, I'm sure. Cooper, on the other hand, just empathized, and then, when I went in to clean out my desk, he marched himself straight into the boss's office and did what I would have done if I weren't a lady. Of course, I'm sorry about the Klez virus on the firm's server, but you have to admit it's pretty impressive for a dog to know how to write code. Anyway, it was a catharsis for both of us, even if the judge didn't see it that way.

Cooper's empathy skills are so acute that I've decided to let him screen not only potential suitors but friends and family members, too—my very own Office of Homeland Security. He's really strict. In fact, it's just the two of us now. I'm pretty happy, mostly, but I can tell that Cooper senses that I'm a little lonely. I think if I really want to he'll let me get another dog.

Lady & Trixie
from *A Blue Dog Christmas*

George Rodrigue

*I*t may sound strange, but when I think of Christmas, the first things that come to mind are not reindeer, mistletoe, Santa Claus, or even the story of the Nativity. No, when I think of Christmas, I think of dogs. In fact, I can't conjure a single boyhood memory of the holiday without the image of a dog appearing in my mind's eye. There were probably about twenty kids living on our end of St. Peter's Street when I was growing up, and virtually every one of them had a dog: there was my cousin's dog, Timothy; the neighbor's dog, Susie; another cousin's collie, who answered to Bobby—I can remember all their names (the dogs', that is, not the owners'). And then there were two floppy-eared terrier-spaniels named Lady and Trixie.

Lady and Trixie were special—more like siblings, in fact, than pets. I was an only child, and these two dogs were my constant companions; they participated in almost everything I did, especially around Christmastime. Trixie came first; she was a black terrier-spaniel mix. Unlike Blue Dog, however, Trixie had inherited the floppy ears of a spaniel, not the pointy ones of a terrier. When Trixie had her second litter, I pleaded with my parents to allow me to keep just one of the puppies—the lone white one. "You don't need another dog, George," was their response. "But Trixie needs a friend," was mine. My logic, or, more likely, my persistence, won the day, and so Lady joined the family.

A few years later—it must have been the winter of 1957 or 1958—we got a heavy snowfall and enough of a cold snap to keep the white stuff on the ground for a few days, which was very unusual for Louisiana's Gulf region. All the kids on St. Peter's Street poured out of their houses, dogs in tow, to build snowmen. It was an unforgettable scene—the first time most of us had seen thick snow on the ground. The excitement was contagious, and I can remember the whole street ringing with the sounds of shouting kids and barking, scampering dogs. Indeed, as the Christmas holiday approached, Lady and Trixie could sense a different type of energy around the house. They would sniff eagerly around the ever-higher stacks of packages and decorations, knowing something big was going on.

I was scarcely less excited. During those early years, Santa was still very real, and I will never forget the sense of awe that would wash over me when I first laid eyes on all the presents spread out before me in our living room, which seemed to be literally bursting with toys. There were cowboy boots, toy guns, hats, fire trucks—typical stuff for a little kid at the time. But the one moment that shines brightest in my memory was the day I received an erector set, the one thing I had been pining for more than anything else. There it was under the tree, beautifully and lovingly assembled by my father (who insisted that it was Santa who had gone to the trouble of putting it together). I played with that set for a good ten years after that.

The presents weren't all for me, however. I quickly made it clear to my parents that Santa had to pay a visit to Lady and Trixie as well, and, sure enough, each of their stockings was soon stuffed with dog toys and cans of food. There was more dog food around our house at Christmastime than there were candy and cakes, in fact. With my help, they'd be decked out in holly, bows, and sometimes Santa hats and coats. They would sit patiently as I purposefully attempted to attach cardboard reindeer antlers to their heads, or place them in gift baskets and dress them in wool ski sweaters. Willingly or not, Lady and Trixie became my mobile holiday art projects.

As I grew a little older, however, this artistic urge began to require a broader canvas. I must have been in the fifth or sixth grade when I first had a real sense that I wanted to be an artist. I could see that I was the best drawer and painter in my class, and, to be honest, I realized that creating art projects was a great way to show off. So when Christmas rolled around, I began to think of it as the perfect opportunity to put my skills to work, and I knew that I had to set my sights on something bigger than turning Trixie into a reindeer. You could safely say that Christmas was the occasion for my first public exposure as an artist; it offered the first opportunity for me to develop a feel for color, form, and design. The holiday began to have less to do with getting presents and more to do with cutting, pasting, sawing, nailing, and painting.

It will probably come as no surprise that the first big

Christmas piece I did was a manger scene. My initial goal was simply to outdo the Nativity scene at our local school by building a more lavish one at home. I remember constructing the whole thing with rocks, straw, bushes, sand—everything but a live baby Jesus. That first year, my "installation" attracted the attention of some of the neighbors and earned me some hearty praise from cousins and other relatives who came around to visit during the holidays. But no one appreciated my manger scene more than Lady and Trixie and the neighborhood dogs, who quickly found a cozy spot in the hay that filled my giant diorama and were content to nuzzle up with the Holy Family and the Wise Men.

The following year, when I heard that the town of New Iberia was sponsoring a contest for best-decorated house during the holidays, I was determined to create something really spectacular. I was in my early teens by then and was old enough to climb ladders and pound nails, so I set about making a gigantic Santa Claus in front of our house. I spent a good chunk of money at the local lumberyard and on lights to illuminate the whole thing. I created giant painted-cardboard presents to put at Santa's feet, and I ended up having to change the configuration of my whole house to accommodate the huge effigy. Lady and Trixie, as well as my parents, could do little more than sit by and watch. When I finally finished, you could see my Santa from a block away, and the city saw fit to award me the second prize: twenty dollars, not quite enough to cover the cost of making the thing in the first place (my mother, flabbergasted that I didn't come in first, protested that the contest was fixed).

In the two or three years that followed, I continued to enter the local Christmas decorating competition, and I always managed to come away with a prize. My real goal each successive year was to outdo what I had done the year before. It was my first experience with one of the fundamental challenges of being an artist—the challenge of constantly having to create something new, something better than before. Sure, I enjoyed the compliments I'd get from cousins and neighbors each year, and I did think of my decorations as a sort of gift to my family and to the town. But, more than anything, these Christmas projects were a gift to myself, and as the thrill of believing in Santa and getting presents began to fade, a finer sensation took its place: the pure, transcendent joy of creation, of making art. This gradually grew to be the very core of Christmas for me.

Still, after four or five Christmas seasons, I think I started to get a little tired of making these huge projects, despite the joy and praise they brought me. Creating all these elaborate yuletide decorations had set off a spark; it had unleashed my passion for art, and soon this passion would be too big to contain within the confines of my small hometown, much less our little brick house on St. Peter's Street. As it was for many of my friends, who would soon have to leave school and find work, childhood was drawing to a close for me, even though I may not have been aware of it at the time.

In the years leading up to my leaving New Iberia, Lady and Trixie remained by my side almost ceaselessly, and their presence at Christmastime continued to be a constant source of joy and inspiration. At the time, I really had no idea that the world I grew up in would deeply inform the nature of my paintings in the decades to come. And it would be years before I could recognize that Lady and Trixie had planted the seeds for Blue Dog, a creation that would, years later, help me retrieve the magic of Christmas.

Misha

from *Disposable Dogs*

STEVE SWANBECK

While church organists rehearsed joyous holiday music and shoppers scurried about in search of last-minute presents, Rick and Susan Rude of McLean, Virginia, chose Christmas Eve to give the gift of kindness to a tiny, very sick puppy who needed a miracle to live to see her first birthday.

The solid white Coton de Tulear weighed less than four pounds when the Washington Animal Rescue League picked her up a few days earlier from a breeder who kept the starving animal locked in a bird cage in a dark cellar and fed her kitty litter to keep her quiet. The breeder knew there was little chance of selling the dog, who, if healthy, could fetch a hefty price, because she was seriously ill. So the dog just wasted away in the cage, lying in her own urine and feces, until someone alerted authorities. "They just put her in there to die," says Rick. "Her chances of survival were virtually nil."

Rescuers took the anxious, helpless puppy, later named Misha, to a veterinary hospital where doctors determined her heart was defective, but the exact nature of the illness could be determined only through extensive testing. Shelter workers fed Misha as much real food as she could handle, cleaned her up and then crossed their fingers. Coincidentally, or perhaps inexplicably, Rick contacted the shelter at the same time to make a contribution. Earlier in the year he and Susan adopted a Coton de Tulear and a silky terrier mix from the shelter and wanted to express their gratitude. During their conversation, the league's executive director told Rick about Misha, a frightened little dog who probably didn't have much time to live. Rick and Susan agreed the sweet, mistreated animal deserved the opportunity to experience comfort and love, even if only for a short time. "We'll take care of her for as long as she needs care," he thought. "This is something my wife and I feel we should do."

The day before Christmas, Rick and Susan adopted

Misha and took her directly to their own veterinarian, who stayed open longer than planned to help out. The examination results stifled the season's merriment. "We expected her to die any day," says Rick. Nonetheless, they decided to make an appointment with a cardiologist to see if something more could be done. In the interim, Susan and Rick took the frail puppy home and fed her tiny portions of special food with a small spoon to try to keep her alive until the specialist could see her. The cardiologist found that one of the valves in Misha's heart was obstructed; what's more, there was a hole in her heart. The only chance she had, and it was a long shot, involved complicated surgery. "The heart was becoming massively enlarged," explains Rick. The cardiologist referred Susan and Rick to the Virginia–Maryland Regional College of Veterinary Medicine, one of the few institutions in the country with the equipment and expertise to perform the surgery.

By this time, many people might have given up; the odds were against them, not to mention the bills that piled up. Susan and Rick already had three other dogs and a cat. Why do any further? "It was the right thing to do," explains Rick. "We're (humans) the protectors of animals on this planet. They give us a lot more than they take."

In early February, after Misha grew strong enough to attempt surgery, she went under the knife in an effort to correct the obstructed valve. It was a delicate, sophisticated operation, using procedures similar to those that doctors employ on babies . . . and it worked. The surgery went so well, "it was almost textbook," says Rick. Next, the hole in Misha's heart needed to be closed. A month later, Misha went in for her second surgery. That, too, proved successful. "She is now about as fixed as humanly possible," says Rick, who gratefully acknowledges that all of the people involved with Misha's care went out of their way to help her.

Today, Misha is healthy and looking forward to a long and happy life. "She's a survivor," says Rick. "This dog has been an absolute gift." Misha's doggy pals, Fifi, Lila and Angel, make sure she doesn't overdo it as they play together at home. "They get along very well," says Rick. As for the cat? "She sits on top of the dining room table and watches all of them with a great deal of disdain." It's unclear as to how many more Christmas miracles Kitty can handle.

Kate

MARY BLOOM

*I*t was a hot August day when the thought occurred to me. I had been without a dog for a year now and was beginning to miss having one. The pain of the loss of Bree, a sheepdog that I lived with for fourteen years, was in the past. I had always wanted a dachshund; maybe the time had come.

I called the municipal animal shelter in New York City and spoke with Rosemary, the manager of pet adoptions. I described what I had in mind, thinking that my name would be placed on a list and I would have to wait until an appropriate dog came into the shelter. I said I wanted a female, preferably a small dog who would be easy to carry in a bag on trains and buses. As I gave Rosemary my description, she said over and over, "I don't believe this." I knew then that she had a dog there right now who met my requirements. Indeed she did.

Anxiously waiting for someone to enter the room, alert to every sound in the hallway that might mean freedom from her cage was a small red dachshund who had been turned in by an older man. This sweet little dog came complete with bite warnings that had been issued. It seems the dog had attempted to nip and could not be trusted. Due to the bite history, the dog was placed in the "kill room" with others that had done something society did not accept and, therefore, were not to be adopted. Because the five-day legal waiting period had passed, the small dachshund would be meeting an early end and would be "put to sleep." Rosemary had gotten attached to her and had already stretched the dachshund's time twice, but that night would be her last. No one had come along who was willing to take the chance on a possible biter. Rosemary's knowledge of dogs told her this small dog was safe; but she could not help remembering the words of the man who turned her in, and because of the warning, she was not able to put her with the other dogs waiting for homes. Then, on the dog's last day, I called. It seemed like fate.

I rushed uptown on the subway and arrived after the adoption office was closed. Rosemary left a note telling me to go into the "kill" room and I would spot her among the other dogs, which were indeed threatening. Following the instructions on the note I opened the door and immediately looked to a cage where a dark pair of eyes stared at me while the tail at the end of the long body never stopped wagging. I fell in love. She was petite and had a rich red-brown coat that shined like a new penny. Her short stumpy legs supported a long body and she had wide, large ears that seemed too large for her tiny head. Perhaps it was because it would have been her last night or we were meant to be together, I'm not sure, but she certainly appealed to me. She was just the dog I had in mind. As I approached her cage she was thrilled knowing she had a chance to leave and wiggled like a fat worm. Opening the cage door, I picked her up and put her on the floor because she was so lively I feared dropping her. She snatched the leash from my hand and ran for the door, then turned and looked up at me with a look of joy in her eyes and the leash dangling from her little mouth. That moment cut into my heart. It said it all. After signing some papers in the adoption office, we left the building and walked twelve long blocks toward the subway home, all along the way her great enthusiasm pulled us ahead with her tail wagging constantly. I knew then that whatever happened I would never bring her back.

I had brought along a duffel bag that was designed like her, low and long. When I arrived at the Seventy-ninth Street subway station I placed her inside and zipped it almost to the top. With the bag on my shoulder she stayed still, peeking out only once or twice. Somehow she knew she was on her way to a better place. When I got to my building she came through the narrow doorway and tackled the five flights of stairs to my loft like she was shot out of a cannon. She flew up the stairs. I had worried about the steps and her short legs, but determination was a strong part of this little dog's character and the stairs never bothered her for a minute.

After exploring the small loft and drinking water after her long ordeal, I proceeded to give her a bath. She smelled like a dirty cage and I wanted all of that behind us. She stood still in the tub, loving the rubdown with the lemon oil doggy shampoo, and she enjoyed the massage I gave her with the towels I used to get her dry. Just as we were completing the drying, the phone rang. I left her in the bathroom with the door closed. After finishing a call from a friend who I told briefly about my new dog, I returned to the bathroom. She had ripped apart every towel. She was having a gay old time shredding them into bits. I worried when I saw the mess the rugs would be next, along with other treasures around the house. In spite of my fear that she was destructive, she never did that again. Looking back I realized this little dog was overcome with joy at that moment, she was a fastidious dog and now she felt cared for and happy to once again be in a home.

I dragged out an old dog bed that I got at a yard sale and put it on the floor next to my own. She knew exactly how to use it and curled up after her first meal and more water on this hot day. I'm not sure what she dreamed about that night, but I swear I saw a smile on her small red face, and on mine. I had a dog again.

The days that followed brought learning experiences and insight into her personality. She had a dislike of sudden moves (like small children running by and motorcycles), she loved long walks, and had a great amount of energy, along with lots of enthusiasm for life. I named her Kate, which suited her perfectly, and she answered to it from the first call. She was such a good example that size did not matter. At only ten pounds she wanted to do it all. I never saw any evidence of her nipping or dislike of anything that would cause her to snap, which was the very reason she was supposed to have been brought to the shelter in the first place. I loved this dog and the new meaning she brought to my days.

About a month after I got her, I got a job assisting a photographer who was going to be filming fancy doghouses on someone's property in Rye, New York. I was going to be gone for a very long day, and because I was hesitant to leave Kate alone, I asked if she could come along. I was told she was welcome and that she could also model for one of the doghouses. The film crew was picked up early in the morning, and we made the hour-and-a-half trip to Rye in a fancy black Lincoln Town Car. Kate was riding on my lap looking out the window most of the way.

When we arrived I had my work to do. Not wanting Kate to be in the way of the crew, I approached Teddy Stillman, the man who would be tending to our needs while we were working on the grounds. The property belonged to his employer, Mrs. Egan, an older woman who lived in a mansion in the distance. She was willing to let the film company use her property (which consisted of acres of land touching on Long Island Sound) for the day. Teddy was the groundskeeper and he loved dogs. He agreed to keep Kate with him while I did my job that day.

When I could take a break I noticed Kate rushing about the property. She was even going in the water to chase a ball. At the time, I did not know she loved to play with balls so much. She was also off a leash on this fenced property, unlike in the city park where I walked her each day. She obviously loved to run. Teddy and Kate were having a great time together. Every so often she rushed over to me to make sure I was there and to show me her ball. It was a good day for Kate and I learned that those small legs never seemed to tire of chasing toys.

As the film crew packed up at the end of the day, we were told that Mrs. Egan wanted to meet us in the mansion. I was going to stay behind with Kate but in fact it was the dog Mrs. Egan most wanted to see. In earlier years she had lived with dachshunds and seeing that little dog rushing about her property reminded her of the dogs of her past and the pleasure they brought. Once in the mansion, Kate immediately found a ball under a radiator that had been left there about twenty years before by Heidi, the dachshund of the house at that time. Mrs. Egan fussed over Kate and took her on her lap. The dog was so tired from her long day rushing about that she fell asleep. They were a sweet couple and the woman looked thrilled. She asked about Kate's history and was shocked to hear she was from a shelter and that someone actually turned her in to die.

Mrs. Egan invited me back with the dog whenever I wished to visit and I knew she was sincere. I think Kate had the time of her life that day and it was that which led me to say, "Would you like to keep her?" Mrs. Egan was shocked and so was I when I said it, but how could I not do what was best for this dog and give her to an old lonely woman who had so much property that the dog would never tire of things to do. I told Mrs. Egan to think about it and I would as well.

All the way home members of the crew questioned how I could consider giving up Kate. As sad as it made me, I felt she would have a better life in the mansion than she would in one small loft at the top of five flights of stairs in New York City. I would miss her, but I would get over it knowing she had a better life than I could provide. I owed it to her.

The next morning I got a call from Mrs. Egan, and we set the date to bring Kate back. I delivered her the following day. I wanted to get it over with, as I was terribly sad. Winter was coming to New York, and knowing Kate was going to go on a holiday to Florida with a lonely old woman for the chilly months and not know the cold again was my comfort. Dachshunds are not built for snow.

A friend came along for the ride and we hardly spoke. Kate bounded out of the car when we arrived at the mansion, remembering her romp there a few days before. She ran into the house and hardly heard my goodbye. After a brief visit with Mrs. Egan, showing her how to care for Kate, I just turned around and left. The rest of that week and many weeks that followed were lonely and strange. My only contact was one call I got from Mrs. Egan thanking me for the dear little dog. They were pals and Kate was having a good time.

Several months passed and the Christmas season came alive in the city. The weather turned freezing and the snows came. I decorated the loft and went to hear concerts and carols. I did volunteer work here and there trying to get in the "mood." I have never been a huge fan of this holiday, not since childhood. All the gift-giving seemed wasteful and overdone. Then something happened to change my feeling about Christmas forever. I got a call from Mrs. Egan's housekeeper, Emily. Mrs. Egan was away in Florida and could not keep Kate. The facility where she was staying all winter was not willing for a dog to come, so Kate had been left behind. Emily took care of her, but Kate was clearly unhappy. Now Emily was down with the flu and the dog was neglected so she thought I should come. In fact, Emily confessed she never thought the large house with lots of toys and room to run ever made the dog happy. Mrs. Egan was ill most of the time and Kate did not really have a friend there as she had in me. Yes, she had toys and space and a food bowl with her name on it along with a lot of servants in the house who took care of her, but I learned that she soon lost the sparkle she had in the beginning. She would not even play ball.

I rushed up to the house not knowing what to expect when I arrived. Maybe Kate was sick or had forgotten me. When the door opened the little dog was so happy to see me she nearly went out of her mind. She leaped high in the air and turned circles around me at least ten times. She was overjoyed! I sat on the floor with this commotion going on and felt happier than I could ever remember. I spontaneously laughed and laughed. Kate jumped in my lap and kissed my face over and over. She even chewed on my ears and hair. Emily was speechless and knew that calling me was the right thing to have done. I hugged and thanked her, put Kate's red wool sweater on and left.

Back in the city Christmas took on a new meaning. Now I really heard the music and felt the spirit of the wonderful holiday. I had just gotten the best gift I could ever remember—the love and devotion of a little dog who needed me as much as I needed her. Kate kept her eye on me everywhere I went, perhaps afraid that we would part again.

We had twelve Christmases together after that wonderful reunion. She loved me, and was with me constantly. In return I promised her that she was my dog, a best friend, and that we would always be together. I would never part with her again.

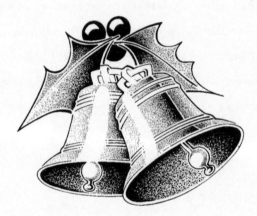

Guests
for the Holidays

TEOTI ANDERSON

><++>+O++>+<

*M*y pet-sitter canceled! I know you said before that you wouldn't mind keeping Cider, but are you sure? I hate to ask, but we're leaving tomorrow!" my friend asked.

"No problem!" I replied. "What's one more?"

I had already arranged to keep another friend's dog while she traveled over the holidays. And even though I knew I would have a full house considering I'm a single woman with three dogs and one cat of my own, I wasn't worried. My pets were used to visitors and since my friends were also assistants for my dog-training business, I knew their dogs were pretty well behaved.

Pippin, my nine-year-old papillon, would probably

feel the most put out. Pippin was often offended at the slightest hint of another creature occupying the center of the universe. Whenever his place in the cosmos was in doubt, he felt a burning need to remind me that he was, truly, the most affectionate, most adorable, most important animal in my life. He would hurl his seven pounds into my lap and shower my chin and ears with a flurry of frantic kisses. "You love me best, right? Me? Me? Me?" Lucky for him, my other furkids didn't mind sharing.

Black Labrador Logan was just over a year old, bursting with bounce. He swam through life like a baleen whale—jaws wide open and ready to snag anything in his path. Logan adored Pippin, racing to greet him every morning and offering an affectionate slurp. Pip, to say the least, did not share the love. Since Logan was the baby of the family, and an active one at that, he often required a lot of my attention. Pippin didn't appreciate having to share that commodity, except when it came to my other black Labrador, Cody. Cody was already with me when Pippin joined the family, so the papillon grew up with Cody as his best friend.

Cody was my dear old man. A sweet, snow-faced eleven-year-old, Cody had started life as a stray. He suffered an accident at a tender age and, as a result, had to have his front left leg amputated. I adopted him from my veterinarian soon after the surgery. He never missed the leg growing up, but in these twilight years we were paying the price as arthritis settled into his joints. He still had the heart of a puppy, but his body could no longer keep up with the youngsters. My biggest concern in pet-sitting other dogs was in keeping Cody and his achy bones safe. I figured with all the dog crates and baby gates I had on hand, I could separate animals as necessary and manage the menagerie.

Baby gates would also come in handy for Sebastian, my tabby cat. If my friends' dogs proved too rambunctious, Sebastian could leap over a strategically placed baby gate to peace and quiet. He had perfected this technique while developing his favorite game, Torture the Lab Puppy. The game would begin with him leaping out from under the coffee table and pouncing upon the tempting target of Logan's constantly in motion tail. Logan would then gleefully pounce back. A brief wrestling match would ensue, until Sebastian would bolt. Of course, Logan would chase. At that point Sebastian would leap over the nearest baby gate, land with a soft thud, and immediately start bathing himself, for all appearances forgetting the puppy ever existed. Poor Logan would stare desolately through the gate mesh, confused about the rules of the game. Being an ever optimistic Labrador, he fell victim to this game every single day, much to the smug delight of my cat.

My four boys and I had a nice little routine. They knew when it was time to get up, when it was time to eat, and what evenings I taught my late dog-training classes. They knew the house rules, and I knew every quirk and nuance of their individual personalities. We fit together comfortably, like pieces of a multispecies puzzle. Adding other dogs to the mix could shake things up a bit, but in the spirit of the holidays, I was full of good cheer at the prospect!

The first guest to arrive was Annie, a six-year-old rough collie. Annie was so beautiful, you could swear she had her own theme music announcing her every entrance, surging with a string orchestra. A frequent playbuddy of Logan's, Annie had also spent the previous Christmas with us, so she felt quite at home.

The second Annie walked in the door, my two Labradors melted on the spot. They were suckers for this beautiful blonde. She greeted each of the boys, but saved special attention for Pippin. Annie loved little things, whether they were babies, bunnies, or fluffy little toy breeds. She would gently stretch her long nose to touch Pip's, being careful not to startle him. She always looked a tad puzzled when checking him over, as if she wondered if he was really a dog or an animated stuffed animal.

After saying hello, Annie began her perimeter watch. A true herding dog, Annie preferred to frequently circle the house, making sure everyone and everything was in its rightful place. Lovestruck Logan followed her every move, carrying a variety of toys in his mouth as offerings of his affection.

After making sure the house was secure, Annie engaged Logan in a fierce tug-of-war battle. Belonging to a rather verbal breed, Annie punctuated her games with a running commentary. Growls and yips peppered the action as the two dogs vied for the same rope bone. Annie had helped teach Logan this game when he was a small puppy, and it appeared she once again had the upper paw.

Suddenly, a lightbulb went off over the Labrador's head—he was now heavier than she was! Logan discovered if he collapsed on the ground and held fast, Annie couldn't budge him an inch. So he planted himself in the middle of the living room, teeth locked onto the bone, and tail wildly spinning in circles as Annie tugged to no avail. This challenge lasted forty-five minutes! Annie finally had enough, relinquished the bone, and resumed perimeter patrol duty.

During the game, I had settled onto the couch with a magazine, joined by the ever-needy Pippin and Sebastian, who surveyed the action with superior humor. Logan tried to engage Annie some more, but finally tired of following her around the house. He plopped down at my feet next to Cody. It was settling into a nice, peaceful afternoon with my animal friends.

Soothing quiet . . . *Thump! Thump! Thump!* Peaceful silence . . . *Thump! Thump! Thump!*

I looked down. Every time Annie passed the Labradors, their tails thumped the floor in unison as the sable-and-white vision passed before them. When she would disappear around the couch, the tails ceased. We spent much of the next hour with synchronized tail thumping passing the time, until Annie settled down for a nap.

We were all rested when our last-minute guest arrived. Cider, a yellow Labrador, was a tomboy. She was a rough-and-tumble girl, with boundless energy despite the fact she was a middle-aged six-year-old. She, Logan, and Annie were good friends, but she had never stayed at my house before. I was a bit concerned that she would bowl Cody over with her enthusiasm, so I decided to play it safe and put him up and out of harm's way the first night.

If Cider had theme music to her entrance, it would be a rousing marching band number. She came bursting into the house, slammed Logan with a hello and began sniffing around and getting her bearings.

I was concerned that Cider might be stressed, as this was her first sleepover. I could not have been more wrong. She was so comfortable, she got the "zoomies." She got this crazed look in her eyes and dashed off at top speed, with Logan in hot pursuit. Annie, not one to miss a herding opportunity, brought up the rear, barking instructions. The three big dogs were having a blast running full-tilt around my living room . . . a living room that was never meant to be an arena for this sport!

The dogs careened into furniture and bounced off the walls. Since Cider wasn't familiar with the terrain, she kept zooming into places and getting stuck. It's pretty embarrassing trying to zoom properly when you have to keep backing out of dead ends.

I finally called a halt to the shenanigans, afraid that my neighbors would think that I was hosting a wild holiday party. I told all the dogs it was time to settle down.

Cider promptly leaped up onto the couch. Now, the house rule was that big dogs were not allowed on the furniture. Since Cody was on strict veterinarian's orders to not jump and aggravate his arthritis, he wasn't allowed on the furniture. Therefore, no big dogs were allowed, in order to be more fair. (The smaller animals got away with it for several reasons. Sebastian would have engaged his feline deafness—pretending he didn't hear me tell him to get off. Pip was insecure enough that I thought he could use the boost in height, if not self-esteem. And I'm embarrassed to admit this as a professional trainer, but I was unduly influenced by the fact that both of the little guys were awfully cute.)

I told Cider "Off" and she looked confused, but did as I asked. She then plunked her head on my leg, pleading with me to change my mind. She was allowed on the couch at her place, what was the problem here?

"Sorry, sweetie, but no deal," I said. Cider looked crushed. She paced for a few minutes, occasionally plunking her head back on my leg, looking pathetic, and hoping I'd come to my senses. After this didn't work, she finally settled for Cody's nearby dog bed. She threw herself upon it with a melodramatic sigh and immediately fell asleep. I thought that would be a good idea for us all, so I put everyone and myself to bed.

The next day after breakfast, I figured it would be a good time to introduce Cider to Cody. I grabbed a handful of treats to serve as distractions. I prepared to use Cider's "Easy!" cue. I braced myself in case I had to deflect an exuberant Cider greeting. After preparing for a dozen possible scenarios, I felt ready.

I brought my sweet old man out to meet the tomboy . . . who vanished, to be replaced by a silly, flirty girly-girl! With one look at Cody's salt-and-pepper face, Cider was in love. You could practically see cartoon hearts popping like bubbles over her head. She bowed, she danced, she lovingly burped in his face (a Labrador sign of affection). Ever the gentleman, Cody kissed her sweetly then went and lay down in his favorite spot.

Cider refused to leave his side. Logan brought her toys and kissed her ears, but she wasn't interested. She only had eyes for Cody. She darted off, found a bone, and giddily dropped it on Cody's head (another Labrador sign of affection). Cody just wagged, looking quite pleased that he'd landed himself a younger woman's attention.

Since I had to prevent Cody from roughhousing, Cider eventually grew tired of him just lying there and not accepting her flirty invitations to chase her. So she finally settled for Logan. Round and round and round the living room they went, occasionally stopping for games of Lab wrestle aerobics or dramatic teeth clashing. An unknowing visitor would think the dogs were trying to kill each other, but they were having a grand time.

Meanwhile, Annie was commencing her perimeter patrol, occasionally joining in on the Labrador Olympics. Pippin and Sebastian thought it safer to head to higher ground and perched behind my head on top of the couch pillows. During patrol, Annie would often pause to check on Pippin, as if to make sure his batteries had not run out.

The dogs did not leave me out of the fun. One by one they'd bring me toys to throw, or just stop by for an ear scratch and a kiss on the nose. I called these affection breaks, and without fail they were always attended in pairs:

Logan and Pippin
Cody and Pippin
Annie and Pippin
Cider and Pippin

Did I mention Pip had some security issues?

The week passed, with all of us falling into a new routine. I taught all the dogs to wait by the door until they heard their names as cues to enter or exit. (An early attempt by the canines to all gallop through the door at the same time had not made for a pretty holiday picture.) Annie made sure we were all in place. Logan got his exercise running from collie to Labrador. Sebastian supervised from a lofty position, occasionally swatting at a passing tail. Cider professed her undying love for Cody. And Pippin made sure I got enough butterfly kisses so I couldn't lose his little self in the crowd. Before I knew it, my friends had returned, and after hugs and holiday wishes, my guests went home.

When I returned to work, several of my coworkers looked at me strangely when I described my week with my four-legged guests.

"You had all those animals at your house? By yourself? Didn't it drive you crazy?" they asked.

As I listened to their tales of braving holiday traffic, enduring the stress of visiting family and suffering through shopping malls in search of perfect gifts, I couldn't help but smile. What better way to share the season of giving than with animals, who give so much of themselves?

That Christmas was special. As the dogs played and snuggled and acted silly, their joy bounded through my home. I still hear the happy echoes of that holiday, now that Annie and Cody are gone. Annie died unexpectedly a year later, and Cody crossed the Rainbow Bridge soon after. No matter how many holidays we wish to spend with our animal friends, they never live long enough. But the Christmas we shared together was a precious gift, and a memory I will carry in my heart, always.

Christmas Dog
from *Falling Up*

SHEL SILVERSTEIN

Tonight's my first night as a watchdog,

And here it is Christmas Eve.

The children are sleepin' all cozy upstairs,

While I'm guardin' the stockin's and tree.

What's *that* now—footsteps on the rooftop?

Could it be a cat or a mouse?

Who's this down the chimney?

A *thief* with a beard—

And a big sack for robbin' the house?

I'm barkin', I'm growlin', I'm bitin' his butt.

He howls and jumps back in his sleigh.

I scare his strange horses, they leap in the air.

I've frightened the whole bunch away.

Now the house is all peaceful and quiet again,

The stockin's are safe as can be.

Won't the kiddies be glad when they wake up tomorrow

And see how I've guarded the tree.

A Christmas Dog

originally appeared in *The Guardian* (UK)

AMANDA CRAIG

I never thought that falling in love with my children would also mean falling in love with a dog. Dogs were, if anything, even weirder to me than babies. One of the first things Health visitors warn you against when pregnant is pets; and being allergic to the cats I grew up with predisposed me to avoid animals anyway. But "men love women, women love children and children love hamsters," as Alice Thomas Ellis once observed; in the case of my children, it's not just hamsters but every animal from the Jurassic period onwards. At the top of their wish list was a dog. "Dog" was my daughter's first word, and from then on it never stopped. A relentless campaign was under way, in which stuffed toys, other people's pets, goldfish and even a gerbil was no substitution.

Once my son was out of nappies, there was no resistance left. Our life was no longer our own, anyway, so why not get a dog? Nervously, after consulting various dog-loving friends and the *Collins Gem Book of Dogs*, we hit upon the Cavalier King Charles spaniel as small (very important, because this dictates the size of what you'll scoop), beautiful, charming and gentle. "A London-sized dog with a big dog's heart," one friend put it. After guiltily rejecting the Battersea Dogs' Home option (with children, you want to know what you're getting) we found a breeder through the Kennel Club.

He was and is, without doubt, the best Christmas present we could have ever given our children. However much you may dislike the sentiment surrounding this annual event, the expression on a child's face on discovering a puppy is one of the most extraordinary experiences of parenthood. Amazement, joy, wonder and tenderness don't begin to describe it: each face was three round O's of silent bliss. Like new parents themselves, they took it in turns to carry the warm, furry puppy around in their arms or hold him in their laps, hardly daring to breathe. But they are children, not adults. Making them understand they should not dress him up, put him in the dolls' house or smack him for making small puddles was one thing. Accepting him as a member of the family, with his own rights and dignity, was another.

My son and, to a lesser degree, my daughter, became jealous of the passion he inspired in me. Within days, my three-year-old son would express his feelings with bursts of violence, lashing out and behaving exactly as if a new baby had come into the house. I was always there to protect Lucky, who was actually more endangered by my daughter's desire to carry him around, but it was a horrible time. On various occasions I had to crouch over our poor terrified pup as blows rained down on my back. As a mother, your instinct is always to protect the smallest and weakest, and my ferocity in doing this became a battle of wills. Often, families give up on having a dog because of this jealousy. We were all too besotted with him to contemplate this, but in any case it would, I think, have set them a terrible example if I caved in.

It wasn't until my son was able to express his anxiety that I loved the dog more than I loved him that his attacks came to a stop. Just as with sibling jealousy, being able to make a child feel more important for being the protector, not the tormentor, of another living thing is the turning point. Now my son is, of all of us, Lucky's chosen playmate. They play tag together, chase each other around the park and enjoy long sessions watching videos together. For the youngest child, to have something even smaller and more powerless in the house is a challenge to their moral nature. Without a dog it may have taken my son much longer to learn a degree of compassion, self-control and gentleness.

It's much easier to learn discipline yourself if you're trying to teach it to someone else. Just as parents tend to become better people by conveying kindness, honesty and fairness to children, so my children seem to have learnt these qualities, at least in part, from looking after the dog. All of them can be equally naughty, disobedient and mischievous but although I have to admit my dog is better-trained than my children, the latter have learnt a lot of common-sense through looking after him. They no longer dash out across the road, because this could get Lucky run over. They understand why his poo must be picked up, why it's important to eat well but not too well. Seeing Lucky's siblings wheezing and waddling in the park like fat old men, when our own dog is slim and active as a puppy, is a living object-lesson about what bad diet and no exercise bring about. Every day, come rain or shine, we have to walk him for at least half an hour, and this responsibility (even when resented) is understood as part of the contract between human and dog. Of course, there are also dogs who don't have this contract understood, who are fat, bored, unloved, and whose owners don't ensure they aren't a public nuisance. Our dog is lucky in being none of the above. He has taught us about time, because his life will be so much shorter than ours, and about loving something much less intelligent but no less rewarding than your own species. Above all, he has made my children ask searching questions about what they, in turn, will owe their own children.

How can anyone bear to cut themselves off from this experience? Well, as with kids, some people just don't like dogs. I used to be one of them, so I understand where they're coming from. Also, the expense is substantial: vets, pet insurance and good dried food don't leave you change from £300 a year. Most worrying, once you're committed, is travel. The horror of leaving a family dog behind when on holiday is almost like being without one of your children: the heartache every day you spend time away is exacerbated by not being able to explain your absence. If you hate the idea of kennel, you have to make, and pay for, other arrangements. Health and safety regulations mean that family outings to any number of places, from museums to cafés, are curtailed. Ditto going to stay with people who have their own dog— or who hate them. You can't force your pet on them, however charming, clean and well-behaved you believe it to be.

Set against all this is all that a dog can bring into your life. Without Lucky, I would probably have gone on having children even when it wasn't safe to do so. I don't, as some do, confuse the two, but there is no doubt that a dog, particularly a small one, satisfies the vestigial urge to have another baby. Ours completes the family. Elizabeth von Arnim, J. R. Ackerley, Dodie Smith, and more recently Trevor Grove and Paul Bailey have all written wonderful books about their own canine companions, yet the family dog remains unheralded. I wish it were not so. Children are wiser than we know in wanting to be close to animals, and if having children finds a proper place for the childish in the adult, as Martin Amis observed, so having a dog finds a proper place for the animal in us, too. The Christmas story includes animals, and it is their patience, gentleness and silent companionship that forms one of the deepest kinds of love a family can know.

Hippity, Happity Holidays!

COLLEEN PAIGE

We always had cats when I was a young child and at the age of five, I wanted a puppy more than anything else in the world. Everyone I knew had a dog. All of my friends had dogs. All my parents' colleagues that I knew had a dog. Our neighbor had a dog. And even though that dog came to play often, it wasn't good enough. I yearned for my own; one that I could invite into our home; one who could be the VIP at my tea party; a canine cohort, a true-blue guide in my everyday adventures. The idea of owning a dog became vital to my survival, yet our closet had more stock in kitty litter than Martha sold in ImClone.

All of the dogs that I had encountered at my friends' houses were usually eager and willing to participate in anything we were doing, even if it involved wearing lipstick, being squished into doll clothes, or filling in as Barbie's horse. A dog seemed to be such a perfect playmate. They were rarely independent and aloof like my cats were, and they never talked back, gossiped, or stuck bubble gum in my hair like some of my friends did. My perception of a dog, even at that young age, was of unconditional love.

So I included a puppy on my list to Santa, it went something like this: "Deer Santa, I reelly wunt a pippy. I dont cayre eef he is bigg or smal or has stincy breth. I hop he is poddy trand. Plees, plees plees brig me a pippy." I envisioned waking on Christmas morning, looking out the window onto a winter snow scene. My cozy log cabin home would smell of warm embers and hot apple cider would be simmering on a potbelly stove, while my new dog would be waiting for me in front of the fireplace next to a shovel and a wet pair of galoshes. Of course, this wasn't quite possible since I lived in a big house in sunny Southern California, but a five-year-old can hope. On Christmas Eve morning, I prepared space in my bed for my new friend by explaining in great detail to every one of my ten stuffed animals that they now had to sleep on the floor. I told them that he was a very special gift from Santa and, because of that exalted position, he would be sleeping with me permanently. I went on to explain, with great concern for their little hearts, that he would have traveled from the North Pole and would be very cold, so he needed a warm bed to sleep in. (Was I feeling guilty? I went to Catholic school. What do you think?)

Christmas morning came and went, and the only barking or whimpering anyone heard that day was from me. I didn't get a puppy and was forced to declare Santa "a big jerk." Oh, the tears! I was practically hysterical, like I was just lambasted in the temporal lobe with an Easy Bake oven. I demanded to know why Santa didn't bring me a puppy. The answer my mother gave me was simple: You just don't mix cats and dogs. "Do you want to send your beloved cat away?" she asked. I hung my head and conceded. I couldn't bear to do that. So, as my mother offered me a cup of holy water and a pamphlet on "do-it-yourself exorcism," I sat, still dogless in Beverly Hills.

After I ceased my psychological breakdown, I spied a red Hippity Hop[1] sitting in the living room by the tree

---

1. A Hippity Hop, for those of you who are benighted as to the sixties fad toys, is a huge rubber ball with what was clearly a horse head (but I decided it was a dog head right from the start—you knew that didn't you?) that you would sit on, then bounce to your heart's delight while holding on to the handles.

with a huge red bow around its neck. Mind you, this was no ordinary bow. This was a runway-long, football-field-wide bow that was tied in such a manner that I am sure a sailor would have spewed a few expletives attempting to unknot it. Just as Michelangelo mastered art—my mother was a master presenter. From gift wrapping to lights, to centerpieces and swags, my mother always made Christmas morning feel like we were living in FAO Schwarz. If I could have bottled the smell of our house on Christmas Eve with the welcoming fragrances of sugar cookies, homemade cranberry sauce, and candied yams, I'd put every candlemaker out of business.

With my new toy, aptly named Hippity, waiting for me, I was transported from despondency to heaven. I took Hippity out to our huge backyard and began my mission to bounce Christmas Day away. To anyone watching who did not know me, they would have thought I had downed a whole bottle of cough syrup, I was so euphoric—*Boink! Ping! Bop! Doink!*

On the hill above our backyard stood a large, beautiful wooden gazebo. In this gazebo would lie on a daily basis a Great Dane named Caleb. His partner Nudnik, a Dalmatian, would take residence with him but seemed to prefer to spend a large amount of his time in our yard—especially at night when he could peruse our trash cans. Caleb never ventured out of his gazebo, but any time Nudnik saw me, he would come down the hill to play. As I bounced to and fro, Nudnik thought it a great game and began to chase me. He would jump and playfully nip at Hippity. I was worried that he would puncture my prized toy with his teeth and decided that I had to put a stop to his behavior immediately. I threatened him with spot removal, but this didn't seem to faze him very much, considering he continued to try to disembowel my ball. I threw my hands up, shrieked "No!," picked up Hippity and headed back into the house, thus successfully ending his playful attacks on my precious new pal. When I returned later in the hour, Nudnik was still sitting in the same spot waiting for playtime to continue. And even though I loved playing with Nudnik, all I really wanted to do was bounce back and forth. And again, Nudnik followed. But this time was different. This time he didn't try to bite at Hippity but seemed content to just tag along. I realized then how smart dogs really were, but I still had no idea how smart I was with animals and especially at such a young age. So

Santa may not have brought me a puppy, but I received something just as precious that Christmas. I gained animal insight and this was my first milestone in dealing with dog behavior.

My family finally adopted a dog from a shelter on Christmas Eve Day six years later. I would finally have Fido Food in my closet instead of Johnny Cat. I must have created a persona of responsibility by the time I was eleven for my father announced that I was ready for my first dog. We entered the shelter and there he was. It was like kismet, al dente pasta, and Godiva chocolate rolled into one. I knew he was mine the first time I laid eyes on him. He was a sweet, silky black-and-tan sheltie mix and so his name was born before we even left the facility.

Sheltie was the kind of dog that would look so deep into your eyes that you were sure he could diagnose cataracts or divine any trespasses you had not expurgated yourself during confession. He was playful and pleasant to live with. We never needed to use a doggie door, as he would alert you to his desire for elimination by giving you that look of "Excuse me, but I feel the need to alleviate my bowels of their ever-increasing volume. Can you please allow me to momentarily exit this beautiful shanty?" I always thought that if he could speak, he would sound like Sean Connery. He was such a gentleman.

Sheltie had many talents. When my father was ill and had to be attended by paramedics, Sheltie had to be locked in the bedroom. Not that he was hostile, as he was very friendly to strangers and never gave evidence of an aggressive bone in his body, but, he would need to be right there in the mix, questioning whether you knew exactly how to use that medical equipment or not. He wanted to make sure that you knew, at any time, if you needed his help, he was fully capable of being Lassie. He lived for many wonderful years, and I cried torrents of tears when he passed. He was my first true friend and when I think of him, I cannot do so with a dry eye.

I've had a few dogs since Sheltie, but no animal has changed my life as much as my chihuahua, Tinkerbell. She is not the only dog in my home, but she is the only dog who brought me love. Not just her love, but the love of a man. I met my husband, Stan, three years ago when he called me to train her and the rest is history. The first time I laid eyes on the both of them, I knew I was home. Tinkerbell proved to be a more challenging student, and Stan the perfect client. In no time he had this little tank of a dog under control and wrapped around his finger. As far as me being wrapped around his finger, that was a given. He had me at "I need your help."

Tinkerbell is going on five years old and is quite the character. She is mixed with a tad of dachshund and I'm sure a bit of Tasmanian devil. She has a vast vocabulary, at least seven of Sybil's personalities, and does a few dialects, one in particular sounding like a gremlin saying the name Abba when she wants a Greenie. She has an insatiable appetite. If there is food, she will find it—she will fight a viper for it and win. Like most of us, her appetite is disproportionate to her size. However, if human, she would ride a Harley and wear full leather, sporting Victoria's Secret underneath. She always knows exactly what she wants and occasionally it appears as if she's even cussing at me when she doesn't get her way. Oh no, don't let the name fool you, Stan named her and I'm sure in the deep subconscious recesses of his mind, he wanted to deceive the world about this fearless little creature.

Then there's my black Lab mix, Sailor, who would cower at a baby bunny. She's so sweet and submissive, a rescue dog that was badly beaten. I was volunteering at the shelter when I found her, curled up in a ball in the corner of her kennel, shaking like a leaf. Her big brown eyes beckoned me to take her home. So I adopted her a few weeks before Christmas 2001. I have never had a dog who trained herself, but it's true. She rarely needs to be on leash, loves kids and other animals, and has manners. She is the perfect Christmas dog for photos by the tree. It makes me laugh when I think about how pliable she is. She's like Gumby. You can put a Santa hat on her, an elf on each shoulder, balance her on one leg, and have her spinning angel hair and she'd just look at you as if to say "Love hurts—but it's so worth it." You could have the Griswold Family Christmas Tree, concealing twelve squirrels with T-bones and gingerbread hanging from the boughs and she would not even touch it. Tinkerbell, on the other hand, would have already hired a work crew to lift her to the top of the tree so she could eat her way down.

Christmas 2004 was the best Christmas I've ever had. It was the first one that lived up to that childhood dream from so long ago. I had not one dog but two . . . and I awoke to snow. For a bonus, I had a wonderful husband and a terrific kid. It was obvious to me that it was finally time for that enchanted holiday walk in the snow, which for me was never a possibility until we had moved to the Pacific Northwest. In fact, I had never even seen real snow until I was nine years old. Most of my holidays were spent in seventy-to-ninety-degree weather—weather that guaranteed your tree was almost dead before you even got it home. Despite the lollipop-sticky temperatures endured during the holiday season, Hollywood didn't spare a bulb in decorations. From the Santa Monica Pier to the La Brea Tar Pits, lampposts were strangled with ropes of glittery garland glistening in the Santa Ana breezes. But it wasn't snow. And snow on Christmas was special. I'd waited my whole life for this experience. I felt like I was preparing for a trip to Disneyland.

All bundled up, gazing up into the dark, dove-gray sky, my eyes suddenly became blinded by snowflakes. They were the slow-falling, greeting-card kind of snowflakes that had only existed in my imagination. Snowflakes that were so soft and so petite that in no time they built up on my coal-black Lab's eyelashes, making her look like a furry showgirl.

We started down the path, and I was in heaven. In my excitement to get outside, however, I had forgotten Sailor's bright red ball. When Sailor goes after an object, most people will only see a blur. She runs at the speed of light, a black wisp in the sunlight, a soft dark mass of matter that makes any strip of grass a NASA runway. She will run after most things that are thrown in the opposite direction of her being. Any item, any shape will do—a tire iron, a Q-tip, an eggplant—it doesn't really matter. Whatever moves, she's after it and will bring it back safely.

Sailor gave me a look that blatantly said, "What? You forgot my B-A-L-L?" (I can only spell the word in front of her, because if I say "ball," she acts as if someone just gave her crack.) My husband jokingly picked up a large handful of snow, compacting it into a small snowball and threw it. We continued on, talking and strolling through our winter wonderland when I heard a whimper. Sailor had retrieved the snowball without my noticing and had been holding it for a couple minutes in her mouth. I couldn't believe it. Her tongue was blue but she wanted to play with whatever was on hand.

For forty-five minutes she chased and retrieved snowballs, bringing them back intact. I had never seen a dog do this before. She is either a very clever dog or has severe obsessive compulsive disorder and is in need of some strong psychoactive drugs. Either way, she is a whole lot of fun. Christmas for me has always been filled with magic, lessons, and love. Sharing the holidays—and every day—with the dogs in my life has been an unforgettable experience.

A Blessing in Disguise
from *Modern Dog* magazine

CONNIE WILSON

*I*t had been a crazy busy work week, so it was with eager anticipation that my partner, Doug, and I threw a couple of hastily packed bags into the car and rushed off to catch the last sailing to Salt Spring Island, where the peace and serenity of our weekend getaway awaited. My dog, Kaya, had arranged herself comfortably in the backseat, but as we approached the ferry terminal she, as usual, started to become anxious. A nervous dog, she doesn't like the ferry ride because of the strange noises, the rocking motion, and being left alone in the car while we go up to the cafeteria, but she knows the drill by now and has somewhat resigned herself to this leg of the journey. The ferry thankfully departed on time, bringing us into Long

Harbour close to midnight. After the usual docking pro-
cedure, we finally offloaded. Any hope for a warm, early
spring weekend was dispelled by the chill rain and drizzle.
It was also very dark; pitch black to be precise. In the city
there's that omnipresent glow piercing the darkest of
nights, but not here in the country. We set off on the fifteen
minute drive to the house and Kaya, sensing our imminent
arrival, began to pace back and forth.

Unfortunately, Doug doesn't share the same love for
dogs I do, and Kaya was really beginning to annoy him.
As Kaya checked our progress, pacing to and fro in the
backseat, she managed to swipe her head against the back
of Doug's with each turn. Every few moments she stopped
to look over his shoulder and out his window, thereby
brushing her doggie mouth on his jacket and breathing
her doggie breath by his face. Doug tersely drove on.

The house sits on top of a hill and has a long driveway leading up to it. It's at the beginning of this driveway
that we always let Kaya out so she can stretch her legs and
get some exercise running up the hill. Delighted, off
Kaya went, sniffing, peeing, and barking all the way. She's
a hunting dog, a Weimaraner-pointer cross with an in-
credible sense of smell, and there's certainly many more

interesting things to "sniff out" here than in the city.

Having finally arrived, we unloaded the car, unpacked, and got ready to go to bed. Alas, Kaya was nowhere to be found. Doug convinced me she'd be back soon, so I climbed into bed and lay there waiting to hear the patter of her feet outside our bedroom window. Time ticked by and still Kaya hadn't returned. It was now 1:30 a.m. Where was she? I was *so* tired. I was finally here, away from work and ready to relax; I had finally gotten my spot on the bed warmed up. This just wasn't fair! But love and concern beat out exhaustion and up I got, throwing on some clothes over my pajamas and trudging outside to stand in the pitch blackness and call for my unresponsive dog. Feeling desperate, I finally got in the car and drove back down the hill to see if I could find her. Halfway down, I noticed a deer-like shape running beside me. It was Kaya, happy as a clam to be joining me on what she thought was another adventure.

Finally we were both back inside the house. My side of the bed was no longer warm and it took me another thirty minutes or so to get comfortable enough to drop off to sleep. By this time it was two in the morning. What seemed like mere moments later, I was awoken from my slumber. It was still dark as night and Kaya was at our bedroom door, whining. It wasn't yet 6:00 a.m.; I'd been asleep for less than four hours. I thought about Doug's antique rugs and worried about what could happen if Kaya truly needed to go out. So, I got up again. I quickly let her out and then grabbed a coat and shoes and went out myself. Only minutes had elapsed but Kaya was, for the second time that evening, nowhere to be found. And there I was once again, shivering in the dark, calling for my dog and feeling like I could wring her neck.

But, standing there awaiting Kaya's return, memories of other such cold winter evenings came back to me. Though it seems like just yesterday, I've shared eleven crazy, wonderful years with Kaya.

It wasn't until my marriage split up, and my children and I were on our own, that having a dog in our lives became a possibility. My former husband had been totally opposed to having a dog. Well aware of my fond memories of my childhood dog, Tex, a loyal and loving pointer who watched over my sisters, brother, and I while we were growing up, my daughter Jennifer came home from school excitedly waving the classified section of our small community newspaper. In it was an ad for puppies born from a German shorthair pointer mother and a Weimaraner father. I was, however, unsold; I had less-than-fond recollections of a neighbor's lovesick Weimaraner. I told Jennifer I'd *never* want a dog like that.

Not to be dissuaded, Jennifer came home from school the next day armed with a hefty dog encyclopedia and proceeded to recite all the exceptional attributes of those two particular breeds. She pointed out that none of the other breeds had *half* as many good words written about them. "At least let's go take a look, Mom." Not quite realizing I was sealing my fate, I reluctantly agreed.

The puppies had been born on Christmas Day, and when we went to see them in early January, they were like tiny bundles of brown velvet. I held one in my hand and knew the girls had won. The puppies weren't ready to leave their mom yet, so we departed in deep discussion about the logistics of keeping a dog. Being newly single, I was concerned about adding more responsibility to an already forbidding load. My daughters convinced me that we would all share in the duties of looking after our new dog, and with that promise—one which parents the world over have fallen for—I acquiesced.

With the puppies now ready to leave their mother, we

thought we were well prepared with our training manual, crate, puppy food, blankets, collar, and leash. Little did we know nothing could have prepared us for Kaya.

There were seven chocolate-brown wiggly puppies, so sweet and adorable—how were we ever to choose? While my daughters played with the puppies, trying to decide which one would be coming home with us, I looked over at the mom. Barking and whining and straining at the very end of her leash, she was certainly very different from my childhood dog, Tex. Tex had never been a barker so I had erroneously assumed that quiet deportment was a trait of German shorthairs. But then, maybe she was just concerned about her puppies. Not surprisingly, Kaya inherited her mother's annoying habitual barking.

Any family that goes through a breakup knows all about the guilt, sadness, and heartache that come into play both during and after the split. Adding to that were my fears of bringing a puppy home and not being able to handle the extra responsibility on top of everything else. My fears, however, were quickly allayed. Kaya brought my daughters and me together and helped us through a very difficult time. But she didn't do this through being what people would consider to be a really good dog; she accomplished this through being just the opposite—a really, really bad dog.

Kaya, being very smart (and I think this was more than half the problem) was housebroken quite early and had relatively few accidents. When she was really young and needed to go out in the middle of the night, it was decided we would all take turns. That lasted just one week. My daughters dutifully awakened when they heard Kaya bark, got bundled up, and sleepily took the dog outside, encouraging her to do her business so they could get back to sleep. After that first week, no matter how much Kaya whined they just wouldn't wake up, and so the responsibility, of course, fell to me. So, there we were, just Kaya and I— me, staring up at the stars, wondering where life was taking me, and Kaya, happy to be out, nosing about for the right spot to pee.

Kaya grew into a rambunctious teenager. After letting Kaya off leash, I'd try to get her to come back to me so we could return home. She'd feign obedience until just outside of my reach and then skip away, barking, when I'd try to lunge for her collar. The harder I'd try to catch her, the more spirited she became, running and barking, always just out of reach. Literally, an hour or more could pass like this, Kaya frolicking while I grew increasingly livid, having now become hopelessly late for one appointment or another. Sometimes we'd draw a crowd of spectators who would amass to offer suggestions or just laugh at my predicament. Needless to say it was quite embarrassing.

But, boy could that dog run. There a field adjoining a road we often walked along. I'd take Kaya into that field, unleash her, and let her go. Sometimes people would stop to watch the joy expressed by that long-legged skinny dog as she ran like a racehorse, making countless loops around the field. That unflagging energy made Kaya a difficult dog to contain in our yard, even though our lot was far from being small. My childhood dogs never had to be fenced in; they just stayed in the yard. Not Kaya. She couldn't be left outside on her own for one minute and, even if we were watching, had a knack for escaping under our very eyes.

I lost count of how many times Kaya was picked up by the pound. She had been labeled a "repeat offender" and was on their "bad dog list." Dogs on this list were considered unadoptable and, if given up by their owners, would be euthanized. Every time she got picked up, the fine increased. One of the last times Jennifer had to pick up Kaya from the pound, she was required to identify Kaya from a picture they had taken of her. We now laugh as we recollect the Polaroid taped to the outside of Kaya's thick file—Kaya with a hangdog expression peering out from behind bars. When we'd come to reclaim her she'd explode out the kennel door before they could clip a leash on her, and race toward us, legs splaying in all directions, going so fast she'd wipe out trying to take the corner too quickly.

These antics led us to install an electric invisible fence, in a desperate bid to keep Kaya in the yard. But clever Kaya would endure the slight shock on the way out of the yard, take herself on an adventure and then, upon her return, bark on the other side of the electric fence, having realized it was pointless to get shocked upon reentry as someone would be waiting to let her back in.

Leaving Kaya at home by herself required intricate planning—she had to be kept inside, but had grown too large for her crate, and we were obviously cautious about leaving her to freely wander the house while we were gone. Not only that, but the house was up for sale and needed to look pristine at all times. The laundry room was the perfect solution—it was a bright and cheery room that contained her bed and her food and water bowls, and could be closed off from the rest of the house. Certainly, I wasn't prepared for what I found on my return: the baseboards ripped off the walls and the molding around the door frame chewed and broken as far up as she could reach. Her blanket's stuffing had been removed and there was drift of white fluff everywhere. So much for plan B. Not trusted to be left alone, she now came with us on most outings.

We lived on the shore of beautiful Wood Lake in the Okanagan Valley and when the water warmed up enough for swimming, Jennifer and Jessica would often have their friends over. As most people who swim with their dogs can attest, an exuberant doggie-paddler can leave serious dog-nail welts when treading too closely to human arms and legs. Such was the case with Kaya. She'd want to dog-paddle right up to you, which was nerve-wracking at the best of times, and especially so in deep water. Jennifer decided to remedy the situation by tying Kaya up while they went out for their swim. With enough barking to wake the dead, coupled with you're-not-leaving-me-behind superstrength, Kaya managed to break free and pursue Jen, Jes, and their friends out into the lake. With a good head start the kids were quite far from shore, floating on air mattresses. Jolted from their reverie, the kids were now shouting, laughing, and paddling away from her as fast they could. But Kaya was soon closing the distance between them; having caught up, she scrambled her way up on top of one of the air mattresses, forcing the former occupant off. So there was Kaya, standing on the flimsy, single-person air mattress. Comments from passing boaters carry across the water, "Oh my God—is that a dog? On an *air mattress*?!" And whoops of laughter are heard from the adjacent resort as binoculars are trained on the crazy dog balanced precariously on the tippy surface of the air mattress, barking for all she's worth at the passing boats.

When we moved into a new neighborhood, I built a secure kennel in our backyard for Kaya to stay in while I went to work, yet Kaya still managed to get out. The only way that she could have escaped was to jump, so I made the sides higher. Kaya still got out. While on her daily neighborhood sweep, she'd bring home whole garbage bags from other houses. And once having safely brought her prize home would tear through the garbage, ravenously consuming anything edible (and, certainly, some things that weren't). On one memorable occasion, I ended up with *Hustler* magazines strewn all over my lawn. Other days

I'd return home to find baby diapers or empty cans now licked clean. I ended up having to buy an extra garbage can just for Kaya's garbage. Amazingly, she rarely got sick.

When both of my children left home to travel and go to school, I decided to move back to Vancouver, the city I was born and raised in. After living for over twenty years in a more rural setting, I was a little nervous at the prospect of moving back. Rents were more than double what I was used to paying and, after reading the classifieds, I realized it wasn't going to be easy finding a reasonably priced apartment, let alone one that would allow me to have a dog. The townhouse I had my heart set on didn't allow dogs, but armed with letters of reference from my realtor, employer, family, and friends I was able to convince the property manager that I was a good risk. It was in that Kitsilano neighborhood that I was first initiated into the warm and welcoming network of dog-loving city dwellers; Kaya quickly acquired more doggie friends than she ever had living in the country. As many other dog owners can probably attest, if you have a dog it's hard *not* to meet and talk with people. My fears of being alone and lonely in the city were quickly dispelled with the new group of friends Kaya brought into my life.

But the crazy dog stories didn't end when we moved to the city. In fact, in some cases, Kaya's antics caused more stress than before due to traffic, crowds, and the general busyness of the city. Like the time someone left our back gate open and Kaya decided to take herself out for a stroll through our bustling Kerrisdale neighborhood. After having successfully crossed a few major intersections by herself, she walked up to Waggers, the local dog daycare, and then barked at the door to be let in so she could play with the other dogs. On another occasion, she took herself shopping along West Forty-first Avenue, where she browsed her way through the boutiques and businesses before deciding that the clerks at Payless Shoes seemed pretty nice, so she would stay there awhile, at which point I received a phone call at work informing me of Kaya's whereabouts.

Yet these are just a few of the hijinks that Kaya got up to. Her escapades are just too numerous to recount here. I haven't even touched upon the time she stole the Sunday roast, my dad commenting, "That's okay, honey, I wasn't that hungry anyways." Or when she sneaked into the kitchen to lick the whipping cream from my daughter Jessica's elaborate Danish birthday cake just before it was served. And she's certainly the only dog I know to have been afflicted with canine acne. Memorably, she set to work one afternoon digging up our underground sprinkler system. Or I could tell you of how one could gaze out our kitchen window to see the dog jumping around on the trampoline, trying to catch the bone she had brought up there with her. Or of her penchant for wasp hunting and the subsequent emergency trips to the vet because of the resultant baseball-sized swollen welts on the side of her face. Or her legendary flatulence. Or the photo, still holding a place of honor on my mom's fridge, of Kaya wearing one of the girls' old bathing suits.

Kaya certainly kept us on our toes and would have tried the patience of a saint. There were times that I felt I really couldn't cope with her, but she had wormed her way into our hearts and giving up on her simply wasn't an option. We would train her to be a better dog! After failing doggie training school several times—she had a mind of her own— we were the ones who became her trainees. She's a stubborn, bossy, flatulent barker, but we love her.

Remarkably Kaya's role in our lives became even more significant when she became the muse and mascot of my new business, *Modern Dog* magazine. After demonstrating to me time and time again the lengths to which humans will go to for their dogs, I knew without a doubt that people like me would embrace a magazine such as *Modern Dog*. As I prepared to launch the first issue, my daughter Jennifer returned home from design school for vacation and agreed to help me out for the summer. That was over three years ago and she's still here, working beside me. And recently my younger daughter, Jessica, returned from her overseas adventures and also became part of the *Modern Dog* team. Without them, *Modern Dog* magazine could not have reached the success it has come to know today.

Sometimes we wonder why life throws frustration and difficulties in our paths, but as I look back on my own experiences, I know without a doubt that blessings often come in disguise. Who would have thought that wiggly little brown-velvet Christmas puppy we named Kaya could have changed the lives of my daughters and me so dramatically. Not a day goes by that I'm not thankful for the misadventures my dog Kaya and I have shared. I couldn't imagine life without her.

The Christmas Trip

GEORGE BERGER

D ad was not a touchy-feely guy, not given to open gestures of affection or sentimentality. He was a pretty consistent tightwad, too. So when he announced at Thanksgiving dinner that we were going to spend Christmas in the Bahamas, we were astounded. It was his present to all of us, he said, but especially to Mom, who "deserves a little fun in the sun more than any woman on earth." At the mention of the word, "deserves," Mom started to sniffle; twelve words later she was sobbing.

Dad's little speech, and Mom's reaction to it, was one of those infrequent moments of intimacy that leave kids embarrassed and wishing they were upstairs in their rooms. At least most kids react that way. My brother Pete, nineteen, the consummate sports guy—and pretty much unaware of any of life's subtleties—said, "Way to go, Dad," and reached for the yams. I, twenty-two, a college senior, looked from Dad to Mom to Dad, saw an unmistakable exchange of lustful glances, and immediately felt the sweat beginning to soak the back of my blue oxford-cloth button down. Not knowing exactly how to respond to Dad's *coup de Mom*, I blurted out an echo, "More than any woman on earth." Little sister Becky, fifteen, also tuned in to the sexual innuendo, breathlessly (and uncharacteristically) excused herself and rushed from the table saying, "Oh my God, sorry, I forgot, I have to call Amanda."

Like Pete, Jordan, our black Labrador retriever, was unmoved by the announcement. He sat steadfastly staring up at the platter of turkey—from which everyone at the table had secretly sneaked him a taste during the past half hour—waiting for the next morsel. The only time he reacted was when Dad, now full of pride yet a bit self-conscious, said to him, "Isn't that right, Jordo?" At the question, the big Lab lifted himself an inch off the ground, wiggled his whole bottom, then resumed his determined turkey-watch, that laser beam look of a dog on a mission.

Dad had planned everything: the trip itself was our

big present this year. Then, he said, we were going to do what he'd always wanted, it would be more in the true spirit of the holiday. We'd pull names from a hat; everybody would get another family member's name. You could get a *small* gift, something not too expensive, for that person *only*. That would be it. No exceptions. *One gift each*. We'd open our presents on Christmas Day, in the Bahamas. Instead of the usual gluttony—twenty or thirty presents apiece—there would be *one*. Okay? Okay!

So we wrote our names on little slips of paper, folded them tightly, and dropped them into one of Pete's caps. We picked in order of age. Becky went first; she got Mom's name. Pete got Dad, I got Becky, Mom got Pete, and Dad got me. You could almost see the wheels spinning as each of us started thinking about what would be a great (*small*) gift.

The biggest change in all of this was that we had never been away at Christmas. In memory, the celebrations of the Nativity were, more than anything, raucous affairs at our house. Noteworthy, but not all that unusual in terms of sheer noise volume, was the year I was fourteen. I had finally been given my dream gift, a set of real drums. I remember setting them up right next to the tree and beating them all day long.

It was the same year that Pete decided that he was going to become an NFL star player, for sure, a punter. His major gifts were a Cleveland Browns helmet and an official, regulation-sized ball. He practiced punting to the speedy receiving team (Jordan) all Christmas Day. Just before each kick, he'd take on the role of the referee and let out a piercing blast from the whistle he held in his teeth. Of course, he chose the artificial indoor surface (living room) over the natural turf (backyard).

Becky was only seven that Christmas and, poor thing, she just didn't like any of her presents at all. She had screaming tantrums most of the day. And our Becky could *scream*.

At about three that afternoon, Dad, clearly in an I-can't-take-it-anymore frame of mind, hooked a leash on the punt returner, and left with him for a long walk. It was well after dark when they returned.

On these Christmases past, exhaustion and/or frustration would eventually take their tolls. Ragged and weary, we would stagger to bed. After days of bedlam, our nights fell stunningly silent.

About two weeks before the Bahamas adventure, we all began to focus on the wrenching fact that Jordan wouldn't be part of our Christmas for the first time in his nine years.

Our best buddy, our football-playing, dropped-food vacuum, our honest, big-hearted, loyal to the end partner would be left behind in a dreary kennel while we were on vacation. He had never even stepped foot in a boarding kennel. There was one about a mile from our house, and when we drove by, Becky would say soothing, distracting things while covering Jordan's eyes with her hands, protecting him from the dreadful sight of it. But now Jordan would have to spend a whole week in that very place. Dad had arranged that, too. "I did my research," he said, sounding confident. "It's the best kennel in town, maybe the best in the *state*."

"How can that be?" Becky whined. "It's *ugly*. And Amanda told me they *beat* the dogs in there!"

"Oh, Beck," Mom said, "that's just ridiculous, honey. They couldn't stay in business if they beat them." You could always count on Mother for good, sound logic.

But Becky had her answer. "Not everybody knows about it. They're real sneaky and quiet about it. They beat them at night. And they have thick walls so nobody can hear the dogs yelping." Then Becky collapsed into a choking crying fit as though she herself had been flogged.

Disgusted by his sister's weakness, Pete advised, "Suck it up."

Dad, trying to provide comfort, said, "There, there."

I had to admit concern. I'd said for years that Jordan was my "forever dog," that there would never be another like him. And, after all, there *was* a chance that Amanda was right.

Our flight was at 7:00 a.m. on December 23. Late the afternoon before, we all went to the kennel to check in Jordan and to say goodbye. Becky was sure it was the *last* goodbye with him. I worried it might have been.

The woman at the reception desk was charming and animated. She offered Jordan a cookie treat. He swallowed it whole, and kissed her. She kissed him back. "We give them *tons* of love," she said. I knew I wasn't the only one in the family who was wondering if this all might be part of a setup.

After the forms were filled out and we each shared something heartfelt with Jordan (Pete said, "Go for it, man"), a chubby boy about Becky's age came into the reception area, looped a rope lead around our dog's neck, and lead him to the kennel. Jordan bounced along easily, without hesitation. Mom, the optimist, said, "Look, he loves it here!"

The trip to the Bahamas was in two legs; first to

Florida, then another hour-long flight to the islands. After that, there was a twenty-minute ferryboat ride to the little community and the cottage Dad had rented. We boarded the ferry nearly nine hours after we'd left home. We were tired, anxious about what lay ahead, and worried about what was left behind—our Jordo.

Dad took up a position alongside the boat's captain. As we eased away from the dock, he glanced back at us and asked, "Isn't this *great*?" He asked the same question eight times during the ride (I counted), twelve more times during the first hour we were at the cottage, and an average of fifteen times a day throughout the trip. It was Dad's way of making sure we were *really* appreciating the vacation.

And, in fact, everyone had to admit it was a pretty special place. The weather was consistently beautiful: early morning clouds were burned off by 9:00 a.m., giving way to clear, bright, and what felt so much like *clean* days. Open-window nights were cool and sleep-inducing.

The cottage could have been out of one of those fancy decorating magazines; everything was in island colors— lots of white, and pastel shades of green, blue, yellow, beige. The little house fronted on the harbor; the sea was less than fifty yards behind it.

We spent our first full day wandering around the village, buying groceries, picnicking at the beach, swimming, napping, reading, then eating the meatloaf dinner that Mom made ("a little touch of home," she called it), playing Yahtzee, and turning in at 9:30. Not bad, by any measure. In fact, it was the kind of day most people only dream about. We were warmed, not burned, by the sun; filled, not stuffed, by Mom's best recipe; tired, not aching, from the day's activities. But as I drifted off, I knew I wasn't the only one wondering how ol' Jordo was doing.

Christmas came up as perfect as the day before. Mom and Becky went on a shell hunt, the guys went fishing. We decided we'd try our luck right off the little dock in front of the cottage. What we pulled out of that water were the most brilliantly colored specimens you could imagine. The blue, gold, and green markings dazzled us. Dad caught three, I landed four, and—no surprise—Pete caught the most, nine. We released them all.

Later, some time in midafternoon, a funk set in on all five of us. Dad said a walk on the beach would perk us up. We tried; it didn't. This really wasn't like Christmas at all. We were in the Bahamas, where it was eighty-one degrees, not northern Ohio, where late-December days average less than twenty degrees and snow is more likely than not—that's what Christmas had always felt like. Here, we were walking barefoot on sand, pants rolled up to our knees, the sun scorching the backs of our necks and the tops of our ears that stuck out beyond our baseball caps. We were too hot, too tired, and too sandy. We missed our kind of Christmas, our home, and especially Jordan.

Mom suggested that we have our little gift exchange after supper. So, after a meal of rice and beans and grilled grouper (delicious, but for *Christmas*?), we each brought out one carefully wrapped present.

As usual in our family, the youngest went first. "Merry Christmas," Becky almost whispered, for some reason fighting back tears. She handed Mom a pretty, small, flat package. Mom unwrapped it, gasped slightly, smiled, and held it up for all to see. It was a framed picture of Jordan in our kitchen at home. He always kept one paw on his bowl so that it wouldn't slide away while he ate. (We thought it was just one sign of his superior intelligence.) That was the picture—Jordan eating, his paw on the bowl.

When the rest of us saw the picture, we paused, for

just a moment, then gave Becky a round of applause. "Well done, Beck." "Jordo, The Man!"

Pete was next. A present for Dad, another flat package. Dad opened it slowly, teasingly. Then, for only a second, he looked very serious, as though something had found a hidden emotion in him. It was another picture, of Dad and Jordan on one of their walks, coming straight toward the camera, but looking intently at each other. Dad is smiling. For all the world, Jordan is, too.

I knew, of course, that the third present, mine to Becky, was a framed photo, too. It showed her and Jordan fast asleep in her bed, one of her arms around his head, a favorite pillow in the other arm. Becky, for once, was almost speechless. She just kept saying, "Thank you, I love it. I really love it. Thank you, I really love it."

Mom said, "Well, I guess this is a pattern," and handed Pete another flat package, maybe thirty inches long. I wondered how she had concealed it from us all the way from Ohio to the islands. Pete tore open the wrapping. It was a picture, a wide-angle shot, of his freshman football squad. Through some tricky computer work, Mom had had a picture of Jordan placed in the foreground sitting in front of the team.

"This is the best thing I ever saw, Mom," Pete gushed, "really, the *best*."

Finally, Dad had a present for me. By now, no one was surprised that it was another framed picture. It was a close-up, a portrait-type shot of Jordan. Just under the picture, handwritten, in flowing calligraphy, were the words, "For My Forever Pal, from Your Forever Dog."

And so it was that our deep and abiding love for our dog brought forth five wonderful pictures on a most unusual tropical Christmas evening. We displayed all of the pictures on a long coffee table in the cottage. We all stopped several times during the remaining days to look at them. It made the trip much, much better.

We returned to Ohio the following Friday night. Saturday morning we were all there at the boarding kennel to bring home our buddy, Jordan. The woman we'd met the week before was at the reception desk again. "Oh, that Jordan," she said as we walked in, "he's just a sweetheart. We *loved* having him here!" Moments later, our guy was brought out to us. The reunion was fantastic, all squeals and tail spinning and tears and kissing and licking and hugging.

Just as we were ready to leave, the woman at the desk

said, "Oh, wait, just a second. We want you to have this." She handed Mom a small flat package. Inside was a framed picture of Jordan, romping with his new friends in the kennel's play paddock. It looked as though he was having the time of his life.

Saint Betty Jean
from *The New Work of Dogs*

JON KATZ

*S*aturdays were adoption days. While most Montclair residents were pushing their kids in strollers, preparing brunch, or poring over *The New York Times*, Betty Jean got up even earlier than usual on a bright morning before Christmas. This was one of Save the Pets' prime adoption periods: so many parents would love nothing more than to present their kids with a puppy on Christmas morning. So Betty Jean's split-level was bursting with dogs.

This Saturday she would set up shop outside a pet store. Next week she'd hit the high school's annual holiday musical extravaganza. This wasn't strictly legal; she didn't have a permit or permission, but everybody looked the other way, especially at Christmastime. The faithful Denise, along with Audrey and Maggie, had promised to help out at several locations.

"It's our busiest time," Betty Jean said. "We have to make the most of it."

Adoption days were even more frantic than shelter-visit days. She had to not only feed, medicate, water, and exercise all the dogs, but decide which ones to stuff into her van for adoption.

This presented the usual dilemma. She could bring the hard cases—the pit bulls and rottie mixes people were often leery of—or the easy ones, the poodles, Lab mixes, and puppies most likely to be adopted. Too many of the latter meant the tougher dogs would languish longer without homes. Too many of the tough dogs, though, and people might come to associate Save the Pets with undesirable and unadoptable dogs.

One crate was already in the car, covered by a quilt. Betty Jean shot me an uncharacteristically coy look. "A surprise," she said.

Then she clicked into manic overdrive, racing back and forth with food, water, ointments, and medications, opening crates, letting dogs out and in, cooing, warming, shushing. Adoption days were difficult; she might be relinquishing dogs she had brought back, almost literally, from the abyss.

"It's tough saying good-bye all the time," she conceded. "Usually I can't do it, I can't look at them. Let's face it, we've been through a lot together."

But by eight-forty-five the van was loaded: three cats in cardboard boxes with air holes, seven dogs in four crates jammed ingeniously into the car.

She went into the garage and hauled out a fading wooden sandwich sign that announced: "Pet Adoption Today." She filled a jug with water, put some kibble in a plastic pouch, grabbed bowls, doggie bags, and toys. People loved to see the dogs playing, she said.

On the way to the pet store, she practiced her pitch for each dog. Sammy is a Lab mix, she'd say, who is sweet around women but needs some work around men. Ham is a rottweiler puppy who loves people and other dogs. Stormy, aptly named, needs a lot of room to run and somebody who can spend time with him throughout the day. Pickles, a collie-mutt mix, is a good apartment dog, older and not especially energetic. (Betty Jean conceded that when in doubt about a dog's lineage, she threw "Lab" or "retriever" in there somehow; people tended to see those breeds as friendly and adoptable.) She didn't make up cat stories; people who wanted cats didn't seem to need them.

She pulled into the pet-store parking lot, accompanied by whining and meowing from the rear of the van, and before unloading went inside to greet the store owner, a supporter who always sent her off with bags of food, slightly damaged or returned toys, shampoos, and jugs of odor-killers.

Next, Denise arrived, followed shortly by Audrey and Maggie bringing an older golden retriever who'd recently graduated from foster care. Maggie gently guided him out of the crate and sat down next to him on the sidewalk. He licked her hand, wagged his tail. He had been bathed and groomed for the occasion. The very first people who came by, a couple in their sixties, fell in love with him, and went off to be grilled by Denise and Audrey.

Nobody took home a Save the Pets dog without a long conversation about his or her personal life, habits, moods, living arrangements, and sense of responsibility. Anybody who bristled at intrusive personal questions—and many did—was politely told to go somewhere else for a dog. "What's the big deal? It's only a dog" was a conversation-ender.

This couple didn't pass; their apartment was tiny, they had no yard, and both were in frail health. Betty Jean vetoed the adoption: If one of them got sick, who would take care of the dog? The dog had already been through enough.

Even when Betty Jean agreed, the adoption process took several days, during which a "screener" visited the prospective home and asked lots more questions. It was all carefully designed to give adopters plenty of time to think things over and be sure.

Betty Jean decided a woman interested in one of the puppies wasn't right—not at home enough. The rott puppy, though, went to a young couple from Vernon who'd seen his photo on the website. They had five acres in rural Sussex County. Sold.

An enormous woman in tight spandex pants and with big Jersey hair, a shopper not even thinking of dogs, shrieked with joy when she spotted Charlie, an obese, drooling, elderly bulldog who had already attended a dozen adoption fairs without success. In a minute, the two were embracing on the sidewalk, madly in love. Sometimes, said Betty Jean, things just click.

"Okay," Betty Jean announced shortly before ten a.m. "Now, the surprise." She pulled out the covered crate, lifted off the quilt, and beamed.

"Hopeless!" she declared theatrically, as if for an entire audience waiting in breathless suspense. If she hadn't said the name, the pup would have been unrecognizable. Her eyes were clear, the bandages gone; she was as lively, animated, and friendly as Lab puppies were supposed to be, her tail flailing at every living thing that passed by, two legs or four. When Betty Jean opened the crate, Hopeless jumped into her arms, climbed up her chest, slobbered all over her face. Apart from a few scars where she had been mauled, Hopeless looked great, an adorable dog. And a staggering amount of work. Just how much, or under what circumstances, hardly anyone would ever know.

As if locked by radar, a family of four—the Schusters, Hank, Gloria, and their seven-year-old twins—descended on Betty Jean and the dog.

It seemed a match from the start. Hank, a Wall Street type, worked in the city, while Gloria, a schoolteacher by trade, was at home full-time now, taking care of the kids. There were no other animals in the house. They had a spacious yard and would agree, in writing, to fence most of it for Hopeless to romp in.

They understood that the dog must be spayed after they adopted it, and that if they failed to do so, Save the Pets checkers might repossess her. They readily agreed to the seventy-dollar fee and offered to throw in another hundred as a donation. Without prompting, both parents mentioned the need for professional training to make sure the puppy—which they understood would grow up to be a large and powerful dog—knew how to behave.

This was crucial to Betty Jean; it was the untrained dogs who were most likely to bounce back. She also probed to be sure the parents didn't really believe the two kids would be totally responsible for dog care; she knew they'd be back to watching TV and playing computer games within days.

Nobody looked standoffish, inflexible, or squeamish. In fact, every member of the family was down on the ground, patting and hugging the dog. And Hopeless was in a happy frenzy, licking, chewing, squirming. This was probably more attention than she had received in her entire short but unhappy life—except for the six weeks spent in Betty Jean's care. Another testament to the sometimes amazing adaptability of dogs, given the right circumstances.

Betty Jean handed Hank Schuster a sheaf of forms to fill out. "Let's get the paperwork started," she said. "I think this could work out."

After a few minutes, the twins were saying dramatic farewells to Hopeless, who was going back into her crate and the van until the screeners had checked out the home. Meanwhile, there were other dogs to spotlight.

Hank Schuster had a question about the preliminary adoption forms and turned to look for Betty Jean. But she wasn't there. She'd gone into the van, for "just a second," she said, and was sitting behind the steering wheel, dabbing at her eyes with a tissue.

Whiskers on Wheels

TRISH KING

On December 23, 2002, three vans pull up to the back compound at the Marin Humane Society in Novato, California, a shelter located about twenty-five miles north of San Francisco. About forty volunteers gather around the vans, as the tired, dirty drivers almost fall out of the front seats. The van doors open, exposing crates piled upon crates, each one with at least one dog or cat looking out, waiting for a chance for a new home. The first WOW—Whiskers on Wheels—event is well under way.

Most shelters around the United States are sad places—places where dogs, cats, and other animals are taken when no one wants them. The people who work in shelters love animals, although they get tired after working long hours for little pay . . . and they receive little understanding from the public, which somehow believes that they—the shelters—are responsible for the tragedy of pet overpopulation. Of course, the shelter workers are really unsung heroes, and not villains at all.

Shelters are not all the same. Some are wealthy and some are very poor. Their populations are also quite different. Urban shelters tend to have many large, tough dogs—often used as guard or fighting dogs by their previous owners. These dogs aren't the best pets for most families. Away from the cities, dogs come in a wider variety of shapes and sizes—from hounds to herding dogs (like border collies), to little dogs. Nice, cute, friendly dogs, great family dogs—doomed to die unwanted in most cases.

Deep in the heart of California's farmland is a town called Madera. Its people are poor, and tend to be transient and undereducated. With immediate needs like putting food in human mouths, the residents there don't think much about spaying and neutering their dogs. Of course, the consequence of this is overpopulation, as it is in many similar towns across the country. And, as with other things, the animals' value decreases as the population increases. Each day, when Madera's shelter workers arrive, they have to empty the night kennels, where people drop off their unwanted dogs and cats while the shelter is closed. As the day wears on, other people bring their animals to the shelter, so that "someone else" can adopt them. They have reasons for surrendering the animals—some are legitimate, some less so. Some people are actually quite honest about the fact that they're "tired" of this dog and want to get a new puppy for the kids. And occasionally, as they drop off one dog, family members wander through the kennels to choose another, just as though the animals were clothing, not real living, breathing beings. Of course, many are crying, sad to be leaving part of their family as they move to another town. It's always difficult to find a new home where pets are accepted.

Meanwhile, up in Marin County, years of education urging residents to spay or neuter have paid off and the number of strays and surrenders has dropped drastically in the last ten years. We get very few litters of puppies—in fact, very few pups at all. Most dogs surrendered to our shelter are adolescent—between six and eighteen months old (a dog's most troublesome age) or they have serious problems, like aggression or separation anxiety. Good, caring people come to the shelter to adopt, only to leave empty handed because—there aren't enough dogs!

A few years ago, MHS reached out to Madera, offering to make the three-hour drive down and take as many dogs as we could as often as we could. Thus was the Pet Partnership Program born. We decided we'd take six to ten animals, maybe once a month. Then, as our need grew and theirs didn't shrink, we increased our visits. Madera was always full, always grateful to see a few of their animals leaving for a more hospitable place. My first trip was eye-opening. Each run had at least four dogs in it, sometimes six or more. The dogs didn't necessarily get along with one another, but there were no other places for them to go. The smell of wet, dirty dog was overpowering—the tiny staff spent most of its time just cleaning. They never had enough time to get to know most of the animals, though a few sneaked into their hearts. While we were trying to choose which animals to take, staff members would point out their favorites—dogs that had been there for awhile or were particularly sweet. We always checked these dogs out, if only to make the shelter workers feel validated. Often, the dogs had debilitating health problems.

It's extremely difficult to choose animals from a shelter that is so close to hell. We're looking for sweet, friendly dogs that will be adopted quickly, so that we can bring more in. But most of these dogs aren't exactly on their best behavior—living in cramped quarters, barely having their needs met. Oftentimes, their most compelling need is to get out of the run. Once they're out, they want to stretch their legs and smell the real world, not check in with humans. Still, we do our best. If a dog wants to make friends with us, it's a huge point in his favor. Small dogs are often preferred, just because the human population in Marin is getting older, and the little dogs will speed through our system and out the door. If a dog looks like he's being beaten up by his cellmates, we might tend to choose him. While we're there, we often take note of physical or behavioral problems, and alert the shelter management, which doesn't usually have the time to do what we do.

Still, it's very hard to choose. Some must be left behind. We come home tired and dirty, and feeling awful about those we couldn't take.

In the autumn of 2002, someone at our shelter had what appeared to be an impossible dream. Why not give the Madera shelter a Christmas present? Instead of taking ten dogs and a few cats, why not take *all* of the animals in the shelter in one huge trip? It would give Madera a chance to regroup, and the volunteers and employees could take a well-deserved rest, even if it was for just a few days. We had meetings about the idea, and of course came up with all kinds of objections—where would we put all the animals? Who would be available to process them, and make sure the animals were properly housed? Some of the dogs and cats could stay in our runs and cages, but many wouldn't be healthy enough to handle yet another shelter. Overcrowding and chronic stress cause health problems in animals, just as they do in people. Skin and respiratory issues are the most common, as are behavior problems like anxiety and aggression. Those dogs would have to go to foster homes, so they could begin to recuperate. Did we have enough foster homes? Once the dogs began to decompress, they'd have to go through a series of behavior and health checks to make sure they were safe enough to go up for adoption—would we be able to handle the load?

We made the final decision in November, which gave us about a month to make all the preparations. It seemed overwhelming. It seemed doubly overwhelming to our animal care technicians, who were responsible for making sure the animals were fed regularly, were medicated if necessary, and who had to clean up the almost constant messes. So, we all pitched in. Employees and volunteers who normally did office work got training in cleaning and disinfecting, how to use kennel leashes effectively, and how to handle rowdy dogs, most of which had no experience with leashes and no desire to please their "saviors."

Our foster coordinator spent days on the phone, coercing people into becoming temporary foster homes for the needy animals. Each foster parent has to have a spare room to use for the shelter animals, in case they're carrying a disease. Of course, this isn't a guarantee that their own pets won't catch something, and many do—mostly kennel cough, which is endemic in shelters. Our volunteer coordinator spent most of his time rounding up temporary dog holders and walkers.

Once the animals were processed, they'd need to find homes quickly, so we mounted an extensive PR campaign to publicize the event and to seek new homes for the homeless. We called the campaign WOW—Whiskers on Wheels.

On December 20, 2002, at 6:00 a.m., a cavalcade of three rented vans and assorted cars and trucks left Marin for Madera. There were two people in each vehicle—a driver and a "selector." Each selector was armed with a pen and a pile of control forms . . . and both had a change of clothing. For most runs, selectors' primary job is to pick and test appropriate animals. In this case, we wouldn't be selecting individuals, we'd be pulling all the animals except those that couldn't travel. The vans were filled with crates—big crates and small crates—held together by bungee cords. They arrived about ten o'clock, and everyone got to work.

The Madera Shelter was built to hold about fifty dogs, and fewer cats. As with most shelters, the runs are designed for single dogs—at the most, two. Because of the overpopulation problems, there are often five, six, or seven dogs in a run. This presents problems not only for the dogs—who have to try to get along with their cellmates—but also for anyone who wants to take the dogs out of the runs. Open the door, and the dogs are like children heading for the playground—they all try to force their way out at once. The process of allowing one out at a time can be pretty harrowing, and takes quick reflexes and good handling skills. The dogs are in such a hurry that they often will snap at each other. Sometimes they will unintentionally bite a handler. Once a dog is out and has a chance to relieve himself, he's given a very quick health check, to see whether he has any obvious health problems that should be noted, and a behavioral once-over. We're looking for signs of friendliness—they'll get their real behavior evaluation once they're settled in at MHS.

By noon, one of the vans is filled and on its way back to Marin. By 2:00 p.m., all the vehicles are on their way, and Madera has empty runs, for the first time in years. The staff and volunteers seem conflicted—they love the animals and they'll miss them—but they know the animals will get caring homes in the bay area. Altogether that day, we took over 100 animals . . . most of them dogs.

Back in Marin, volunteers have been alerted and are waiting for the convoy to arrive. As the vans and cars arrive, eager hands are ready to take the dogs and cats. The cats are cuddled and placed in cages. The volunteers take the dogs into our grassy yards, where they can sniff, stretch, and do their business. Then each one is given a collar and placed in a run. Each of the runs has a blanket and toys. Though the runs are still cement and steel, they're all clean—and every dog has his or her own. It's heartwarming to see them investigate their new—if temporary home. Most immediately curl up and go to sleep.

The dogs were all given three days to relax and

acclimate to the shelter, after which they were given their behavior evaluation, spayed or neutered, and put up for adoption. Within six weeks, they were all in their new homes, making their new people happy.

There are many stories about the individual animals— but the most touching of all comes from the Madera shelter's director, a wonderful, overworked woman named Kirsten.

I will try to describe what it means to Madera to have such a terrific relationship with Marin. Every day we look into the eyes of our dogs and cats, and wish they were someone's very special furry friend. Each day we wonder where are the owners of these wonderful pets? For some silly reason, we still have confidence that a teary family will soon come to claim them . . . but it rarely happens.

We encourage adoptions, we take them to all the events our tired volunteers can get to, and we pray for them.

When Marin came to do the Whiskers on Wheels rescue, it seemed our prayers were answered. During the holiday season, when all others are worried about their own, Marin Humane plans, coordinates, and sends a terrific team of caring individuals who spend hours upon hours to help our homeless population. Marin Humane is showing the true spirit of the holiday season, and our pets, volunteers, and crew are eternally grateful.

After the Marin crew has loaded all it can carry, there is a sense of calm at the shelter. We are always busy with many more animals that need help, but we carry a smile for a few days, just knowing that our little friends made it out and are in loving homes. We appreciate all the efforts it takes to rescue these animals and hope that someday it won't need to be done.

Each year since 2002, we have repeated our WOW trip, each time getting better at streamlining our efforts and bringing in even more animals. We also have continued our weekly Pet Partnership trips to Madera and other shelters, trying to help the less fortunate. It makes us feel good—and it makes our many adopters of People-Pet Partnership dogs feel great!

The Christmas
After the Wildfires

Liz Palika

The wildfires that roared through southern California in October of 2003 made headline news all over the world. Not only were the fires widespread—from San Bernardino south to the Mexico border—but there was widespread damage, devastation, and loss of life.

In drought-stricken San Diego county, three major fires began within hours of one another, all spreading so rapidly that within days it was estimated that 20 percent of the county would be burned. Clouds of dark smoke hung heavy in the skies, and miles away from the site, cars were coated with ash.

The small communities of Harbison Canyon and Crest were hit hard by the fires. Numerous homes, small family farms, outbuildings, trucks, and tractors were burned beyond recognition. Although thousands of people, pets, and livestock were able to escape or were evacuated, many others lost their lives.

After the Fires

A week after the fires roared through Harbison Canyon and Crest, schools were getting ready to reopen, and teachers and staff were trying to plan a way to manage the horrors of what had happened. They estimated that one-third of the students had lost their homes during the fires, yet few were leaving the communities; parents had phoned to say their kids would be back. So how to cope with the emotions of such a horrible experience?

I received a call from a teacher, Karen Russell, who asked if there was any way I could bring a group of our therapy dogs to a few schools. She had told her principal how effective therapy dogs could be and felt that if the dogs were at the school, ready to greet the kids, parents, teachers, and staff as they arrived, a lot of emotions could be released in a constructive manner. As the founder of the Foundation for Pet Provided Therapy, an organization that evaluates and certifies therapy dogs, I felt sure I could get a group together, even on short notice, and told her yes, we would be there for the schools' reopening.

I called and e-mailed local therapy dog owners and very shortly had a group ready to go. We had several Australian shepherds, Dax, Riker, Kona, and Dublin; a yellow Labrador retriever, Kelsey; a pug named Gordan; two bichons frises, Sophie and Mindy; a Portuguese water dog, Maggie; as well as several other well-trained, empathic dogs who were willing to give kisses and submit to hugs.

On the first day of school, we all carpooled to the three schools being visited. My dogs, Dax and Riker, and I went to the local kindergarten school. Kelsey, Dublin, Gordan, and a couple of other dogs came with us. We stationed ourselves at the entrances to the school campus so that everyone coming in could be greeted with a smile, a wagging tail, and if they wanted, even some canine kisses.

One of the first people we saw was the school principal. In his suit and tie, he got down on one knee and hugged Kelsey, getting yellow Lab dog hair all over his crisp blue suit. He laughed as she licked his ear. Getting up, he waved away Kelsey's owner's apologies for the dog hair: "The dog hair is a small price to pay for such good medicine!" He added, "I'm glad you're here. Thank you."

Joanne Stout and her Cavalier King Charles spaniel, Rusty, met several parents and kindergartners with hugs and kisses; Joanne hugging the moms and dads, and Rusty kissing the kids. Joanne's warm hugs often allowing stressed parents to shed a few tears while their kids got to laugh and giggle with the friendly dog.

My dogs, Dax and Riker, were busy, too. Riker is an extrovert and feels his job in life is to love people, especially those in need. With so many emotions running high, his heart was about ready to burst out of his chest; all I needed to do was let him get close to people so he could do his job. He stood still so kids could hug him and then he licked their faces; washing away traces of breakfast as well as any tears that fell. But parents weren't allowed to escape, either; if they bent down within his reach, they got loved, too.

Dax is not as extroverted as Riker, and does her job more quietly. In addition, she is very intuitive as to who needs her love and, because she's so good at it, I listen to her. At one point while people were coming onto the school grounds, Dax alerted me to a dad and his son. The dad was holding his kindergarten-age son in his arms, and his son had his school supplies in hand, but it didn't look like they were yet ready to let go of each other. Since Dax wanted to see them, we walked over to them.

"Welcome back to school," I said. Looking at the son, I asked, "Would you like to pet my dog? Her name is Dax." He looked at his dad, turned back to me, and said very politely, "Yes, please." His dad set his son on the ground. As he reached to pet Dax, I told him, "She likes her neck scratched but she also likes hugs so if you want to give her a hug, you can." As the dog and boy got to know each other, I turned to the dad. "It's a tough morning, isn't it?" He grimaced and said, "Yes, I don't want to let him out of my sight." He gestured toward the burned hills surrounding the schools. "And when I see this everywhere I look, it just keeps reinforcing my fears." I nodded, and encouraged him to keep talking so that he could verbalize his concerns. Meanwhile, his son continued to pet Dax, who had slowly and carefully sidled right up next to the boy so that her side was in contact with his. After a few minutes of conversation, the dad stopped talking, took a deep breath, looked at me, and smiled, "You're here for the parents as much as the kids, aren't you? Thank you."

With that he was able to tell his son, Daniel, goodbye

and that he would see him after school; then he left. As he walked away, I heard his son say something to Dax, so I leaned closer. The kindergartner said, "I used to have a dog. His name was Reddy but he got lost in the fire and my dad thinks he may have been burned. I miss Reddy and I'm sad 'cause I don't know if he's somewhere hurt. And our house burned down with all my toys and stuff and I don't know if I'll get any more for Christmas 'cause my house is gone and Santa doesn't know where we live. And my mom and dad are sad."

It took everything I had in me to keep a straight face; I was so devastated that a child so young had to face such life-altering things. But I kept my game face on and let him pet Dax and talk to her until it was time to let him go to his classroom.

As the rescue dog owners debriefed after our visit, we shared stories, wept a few tears, and were all very glad that our dogs were able to help, even if for just a few minutes. But Daniel's comments to Dax continued to haunt me.

Calling All Teddy Bears!

A couple weeks after our visit, Daniel's comments kept resurfacing in my brain and finally I decided I needed to do something about it. I called Karen, our point of contact at the schools, and asked her if we could set up a visit to the kids just before they broke for the Christmas holidays. She was thrilled and said she would check with the school principals and would get back to me. Within a day, she had us set up to visit the Friday before Christmas at the same three schools we had visited after the fires.

So again, I put out a call for therapy dogs. Most of the dogs who made the first visit were willing and able to make a Christmas visit. So the easy part was done; now to the hard part. I wanted the therapy dogs to bring each child in each of those schools a Christmas gift. I couldn't afford to buy that many presents, so how to do it?

Luckily for me, people who own dogs have big hearts! I told the Foundation for Pet Provided Therapy members what I wanted to do, as well as the trainers and students at Kindred Spirits Dog Training in Vista, California, and donations, gifts, and toys came flooding in. In addition, a local hotel asked for teddy bear donations from its guests, specifically for our visit, and the kindhearted guests came up with 150 teddy bears. A local insurance company donated a couple hundred teddy bears, and a group of schoolkids in New York City, thankful for the help they received after 9/11, also donated a couple hundred teddy bears. We accumulated enough so that 650 kids could each have a stocking, a couple of candy canes, a couple of small toys, and a teddy bear. Awesome!

A large group of therapy dogs met at the school to deliver the toys, most of the dogs in Christmas finery. Kelsey wore a Christmas collar with jingle bells; Dublin wore antlers; and Gordan wore a fancy Christmas collar. Dax was all in red and Riker in green, both with bells. Rusty had a Santa hat and Maggie a pretty doggy sweater.

We split up the gifts into groups for each classroom. A couple of dogs would go into one classroom with enough gifts for all the kids in the room. We would hand out the gifts, visit for a few minutes, then move on to the next class. This way we could cover all three schools in just a couple of hours.

Dax, Riker, and I teamed up with Gordan, the fawn-colored pug, and his owner, Sheri Watchstetter. Pulling a wagon loaded with toys, we began handing out gifts to the kindergarten kids we had met just a couple of months ago. The teacher in each classroom helped us play Santa, as did a few parents who were on hand because they knew we were coming. Each child was given some toys, greeted individually, and given a few moments to pet or hug a dog.

In one classroom, I saw Daniel and brought Dax over to visit with him as we handed out toys. They remembered each other, and the eager dog greeted Daniel by snuggling close. I asked him how he was doing and he said, "Okay. We're living in an apartment so I don't have a yard and can't get a new dog so I'm glad you brought Dax by to visit. But Mom and Dad think we should have a new house soon." I told him I hoped his new house would have a nice big yard with a sturdy fence so he could have a new dog friend soon. He smiled in response and hugged Dax close.

Our reception in each classroom was wonderful. The kids were excited, not at all disappointed that the toys were small and were not the more popular electronic ones. Instead, they seemed excited and grateful for what we were able to give them. Toys were handed out—dogs licked kids' faces, kids hugged dogs, and dogs' tails wagged furiously. It was all good, very, very good!

A Year Later

A year after the fires, many of the people in Harbison Canyon and Crest have moved into newly rebuilt homes. Rains have come, grass has regrown, and many of the trees that looked devastated after the fires have come back to life. Although the hills still show the scars of the fires, nature has a way of recuperating and it can be seen throughout the region.

Unfortunately, some of the people who lost their homes are still in temporary housing. They were either underinsured, uninsured, or are having problems with the rebuilding process. Some people gave up and left the area.

Karen tells me that the kids are amazingly resilient and that most are coping well. Other things are on their minds today and, while I won't forget them, I'm happy for them. So although we were willing to make another Christmas visit in 2004, Karen felt that perhaps we should pass on it this time. So, Dax, Riker, and I celebrated Christmas visiting an Alzheimer's facility we go to on a regular basis, and although we enjoyed that visit tremendously, there were a few young friends I missed seeing. My thoughts were with them.

I hope Daniel has his new dog.

Fifteen Years
Until Christmas

NANCY CAMPBELL

We were unwise in our ways when we moved from our rented house on thirty acres to our old farm house on slightly over two. We did not think fencing our old dog in would be needed. After all, he had lived eleven years without constraint. Weeks into living in a home torn apart by restoration, Buck simply walked into the road to investigate the new poodle across it and never felt his passing.

We grieved and planted him properly under the bird bath in the newly wrought herb garden, then set about looking for a new German Shorthaired Pointer puppy. Though I had grown up with beagles and brought home every possible breed of broken dog that crossed my path through the years, Buck's seven years with me turned me into a one-breed person. Only another shorthair would do.

We did the obvious wrong things: we looked in the paper for litters, and we insisted on another boy, "just like Buck." When we got to our first stop, there was but one male pup left. Even as a puppy, he gave whole new meaning to "a face only a mother could love." In spite of the fact that Buck had come to me as a favor to a friend who thought he had bitten a runner (he had not; it was their other dog), he was a handsome fellow and had a pretty good pedigree to boot. I did not care about the latter, but he did spoil me for anything short of classic good looks.

On we went to a breeder situated only a half hour from us. I am easily confused, and the breeder's world, full of crates and cacophony and chaos, made the puppy viewing experience feel like I was seeing the world through the eyes of an adult ADHD sufferer. I left exhausted and thinking we might not find the dog of our dreams.

When I had tried and failed at every turn, I picked up a call from my horse veterinarian. He had an alternate proposition. He cared for the horse of a couple who no longer wanted their shorthair. They raised Siamese cats and a large dog breed, and decided they had too many creatures. Would I take her? They had gotten her from the same breeder whose digs had seemed like canine soup to me, and this eighteen-month-old chocolate-and-milk-colored girl was in a small pen, alone and unwanted, reported my vet. She already had my heart. We arranged to see her in moments.

When we arrived, her minute pen was at the head of the drive. I took no time in securing her in our car, and then walked to the house to negotiate terms. I would not leave her there, regardless of what might be asked of me. I signed a handwritten "contract" scribbled on yellow legal paper that stated a price, and that I would agree to breed her to a dog of their choosing the first time she came into season. I gave that part little thought. After all, I had grown up breeding dogs with my mother. I could do this; of course I could, and I would, to get her home with us.

This began our saga with Maxine. She took some time to adjust, eating the arm of a wing chair that I had just reupholstered, hiding under the bed when anyone came she did not know, spinning madly at the door every morning, and finally settling in regally as she took hold of our hearts and home.

We persisted in our youthful ignorance by thinking we could perimeter train her, but one squirrel over the road later, followed by hours of looking for our lost dog, which resulted in one drenched dress and pair of torn stockings, sent us shopping for a fence.

Once fenced, we trained and grew soundly bonded to our new fair damsel until the fateful time came to "breed the dog." When I saw the strange suitor the original owners had in mind for Maxine, I felt like a protective mother whose daughter was being courted by a heroin addict. The dog was nuts. He raced around like the March Hare, listening to no one, randomly picking ripe tomatoes off of the vines of the nearby garden. I left my girl there in fear and trepidation. When she came home, supposedly "with pup," we waited.

The days dragged by, and nothing happened. Finally, a trip to the radiologist revealed there were no puppies. When we went back to the drawing board, we took a close look at the hastily drawn contract. It said the first breeding would be their choice, but technically this was the second breeding, so I did some research and chose for myself. With the help of the veterinarian who saw our gal to us, I selected one of the nicest dogs I have ever met and have never been sorry for the choice.

I became close friends with the owners of the sire of

Maxine's first litter. They were soon my mentors and taught me the things I should have known before I started my dog saga. I would recommend that every dog owner have a mentor, whether they plan on breeding a dog or not. The experience is invaluable.

A life-changing course of events began with the litter of twelve that fell to my lot. As time passed, and the squirming dozen flowed around my feet in the kitchen, I began to equate these eight short weeks with the joys I experienced earlier in life when I carelessly cared for the pups my mother and I had raised together. The people who owned these puppies became my friends and still are today, many years later.

I kept a girl from that litter, Peggy, who became my first of many show champions. Maxine herself finished a hasty championship winning best of breed over the top shorthair in the country that year. My first home-bred puppy won a series of sweepstakes prizes at regional and national shows. I was hooked. The horses had taken a backseat to the dogs.

Maxine's next litter contained fourteen pups, nine of which were boys. Need I say, fourteen puppies in the dining room between Thanksgiving and Christmas, while both of us were working full time, was not the Christmas we were banking on. A winter litter is like no other. There was the mess of soiled papers in the puppy box when we got home, and the screaming of the hungry hordes. Our dining room resembled a barn more than the room we should have been decorating for the holidays.

Not only is there no possible way to housetrain a winter pup in the icy January and February weather, but the clatter and bustle of Christmas and its bevy of bustle and packages, wrapping and ornaments, food and fancy lights is no setting for puppy "tidings of comfort and joy." People who want a puppy for Christmas should get a cuddly stuffed-toy dog and wait until after the holidays to go and get their new pet. I soon came to think that there should be no Christmas puppies, but the idea is still some part of the American dream.

When the second litter had gone to their new homes, I seriously considered ending my brief and populous journey into breeding. But remember, I was hooked. The filth, smell, and fatigue all faded far too fast, and the idea that I would have a new puppy to love and show made all the work seem small. I never again, however, dared to have a winter litter.

When Maxine's daughter Peggy had finished her time of showing, I selected a sire for her eleven bouncing get. Maxine, however, was not satisfied to sit by as a simple grandmother. Like the stalwart supermom that she was, she quickly melted into false pregnancy when the pups were born, and each time she looked over the side of the whelping box at her daughter's eleven, she dripped milk on the floor.

We gave her half of them. The world was a happy place. New pups went on to new homes, our dog family grew, friendships abounded, and my world expanded further into what is known to the few as "the sport of dogs."

We hunted and showed and trained for obedience, and Maxine finished her companion dog obedience degree in the rain. She lost a few points on her down stay, however, by gradually scootching on her belly to get under the grooming table in the ring during the downpour. She was always smarter than the people around her.

She was mother of twenty-six pups in just two litters, a best of breed winner, an obedience dog, mother of many champions, and grandmother of many more. Never have I had another diligent dog mom, nor such a fine companion.

As she grew older, she seemed never to gray, and some of our puppy folk who came back to our yard year after year for puppy birthday parties would call her "Miss Clairol." She remained the queen of our growing dog pack, and she went unchallenged.

She passed her fifteenth birthday in October as the winter came on us that bitter year. We were engaged by a busy life and surrounded by many dogs, a cat or two, and pounds of show ribbons and trophies. And it all began coming our way that day when we decided to take an unwanted dog from a small solitary kennel in a stranger's yard. She never had a sick day, had no surgery but her neutering, and remained the ruler of our lives for more than fifteen years.

As Christmas approached that year, we stayed close, asking in nearby neighbors for a sumptuous and festive meal in the same dining room where so many had been born. They brought their two shorthairs that they had gotten from my rescue, and embarrassed me with how well behaved theirs were by comparison to my own dogs, as they rested solidly on down stays just outside of the open dining room door while we ate. We exchanged gifts, with all the best and creative ones going to the dogs. We carefully preserved the leftovers with just a nibble or two of roast beef to each of our little pack, and settled in to enjoy the fullness of the moment, the glint of the tree lights, and the snoring of our comfortable pack.

It was time for "last outs" and lights off, so off scattered the herd into that frost of night, and each pattered back, one by one, all but Maxine. Finally, I called to her, and slowly, ever so slowly, she toddled up the drive and into the kitchen.

We thought that she did not look right. I bundled her into my parka and settled her on the old L.L. Bean dog bed in my arms. One by one our dogs and cats gathered around us, like spokes in a living wheel, and lay down. All was calm, all was bright. Forty minutes later, she gave a last peaceful sigh and left us behind. She chose Christmas for her passing—a good time to make sure we would remember. She was always smarter than the people around her.

She was surrounded by her generations and her human family and the occasional cat. Her Christmas gifts, her collar ribbon were all around her, too. Her timing did not make us morose. A good long life is as well ended as it is begun. She was the beginning of a dream, and down from her came our multiple best in show number-one shorthair, agility and obedience dogs of merit, a search-and-rescue dog, and many, many happy homes full of loving dogs. In the very long run, she was, indeed, our Christmas puppy.

We will soon come to the end of our long journey of breeding dogs. I have grown old enough myself to know that I should lay down this responsibility and move on with others. Maxine is also in that now very populated herb garden with others of our dogs that have left us across these rich years. She was the beginning of it all, and her leaving us on Christmas only enhanced the treasury of experiences and proud moments she had always given us through her own accomplishments and those of the dogs down from her. We will miss her, and never forget to toast her life every Christmas night.

Fleas Navidad Nibblers *and* Yappy New Year Yum Yums

FROM THE *THREE DOG BAKERY™ COOKBOOK*

MARK BECKLOFF AND DAN DYE

Fleas Navidad Nibblers

Bakes 16 festive holidog muffins

'Twas the night before Christmas, and all through the house . . . Except for the dog eating these off the counter.

2 tablespoons honey

2¾ cups water

¼ cup unsweetened applesauce

⅛ teaspoon vanilla

1 egg

½ cup chopped peanuts

4 cups whole-wheat flour

1 tablespoon baking powder

1 tablespoon cinnamon

1 tablespoon nutmeg

- Preheat the oven to 350 degrees Fahrenheit.

- In a bowl, mix together the honey, water, apple-sauce, vanilla, and egg.

- In a separate bowl, mix the peanuts, flour, baking powder, cinnamon and nutmeg.

- Add the wet ingredients to the dry ingredients and stir, mixing well.

- Spoon into a greased muffin tin, filling each cup two-thirds full. Bake for 35 minutes. Cool and store in a sealed container.

Yappy New Year Yum Yums

Makes 12 stroke-of-midnight scrumptious snacks

Help your dog keep his rrrresolutions with these low-fat lip-smackers.

2 tablespoons honey

2¾ cups water

¼ cup unsweetened applesauce

⅛ teaspoon vanilla

1 egg

4 cups whole-wheat flour

1 cup dried apple chips

1 tablespoon baking powder

1 tablespoon cinnamon

1 tablespoon nutmeg

- Preheat the oven to 350 degrees Fahrenheit.
- In a bowl mix together the honey, water, applesauce, vanilla and egg.
- Combine the flour, apple chips, baking powder, cinnamon, and nutmeg in a separate bowl and mix thoroughly.
- Add the wet ingredients to dry and mix well, scraping sides and bottom of bowl to be sure no dry mixture is left.
- Spoon into a greased muffin tin, filling each cup three-quarters full. Bake for approximately 1 hour. Cool and store in a sealed container.

Recipes should be considered supplements to your dog's regular diet, not replacements. Consult your vet if you have any questions regarding a particular recipe for your dog. For more information on Three Dog Bakery, please visit www.threedog.com·

Neighbors
from *Dog Is My Co-Pilot*

MICHAEL PATERNITI

The West End Cemetery is full of old dead sea captains and soldiers from the War of 1812, kids who died of cholera, and wives who, after six or eight or ten children, just gave up. There are rich people under monuments, the Longfellow family in a vault, and paupers without so much as a wooden marker. No one's been buried here since the middle of the [twentieth] century and so the place has fallen into disrepair. You see a lot of the marble and shell headstones in puzzle pieces on the ground or standing at crooked attention. About ten years ago the cemetery was a popular hangout for prostitutes and junkies—but now it's just dogs and their owners.

When I first moved to town a couple years ago with

my girlfriend, Sara, we walked our dog in the cemetery. There was this guy there named Jeff, a big brawny American Indian, from the Duckwater tribe I think, who sort of qualified as my first friend in Portland. He told me how he grew up in Nevada and was adopted by white parents and then raised in a little redneck town where people really didn't like Indians. He'd moved around a lot and I pictured him as I was now, the stranger in a strange place. He walked with me in the cemetery, sometimes twice a day, whatever the weather. Or rather, we were both being walked by our dogs. His was a wolf mix named Keana, with a vacant, slightly menacing glint in her eye, who liked to rough up young puppies. And mine is a simple mutt named Trout, whose passion for chasing squirrels follows her lifetime commitment to rolling in poop.

It seemed like Jeff was always at the cemetery, sometimes up to eight hours in a row. He said he worked at night, supposedly for a local scuba diving outfit, and that's why he had so much free time during the day. He told stories, endless stories, about his high school football exploits and the blown-out knee that ended his college career at safety. He talked about fishing, how he gill-netted in the rivers of southeast Alaska and then how he and his girlfriend had bought a house and now they weren't together anymore, and she had the house and he was here, a country away, walking his dog with people like me. He didn't seem angry at all. No, in fact, he seemed happy. Like every day he was as happy as he'd been the day before. And because of it he was good at drawing people out, at connecting the various factions inside the cemetery so that everyone stood around, nodding dumbly, listening to Jeff, our oblivious mayor, holding forth on Keana's new collar or perfect shampoo, while Keana took her pound of flesh out of some hapless pup.

This is not the way things normally work in the cemetery. The mere fact that I knew Jeff's name was unusual. Usually people didn't interact that much. Instead, we knew each other by handles. There was Dalmatian Man, father of three speckled dogs, one to whom he spoke in sign language. There was Greyhound Lady, regally walking her trio of greyhounds until the day that Lightning, her beloved, dove through a plate-glass window during a thunderstorm and died. There was the man who walks and reads, and Frisbee Dude,

and the Lawn Chair Family: an old father and his fifty-
something son who daily set up their folding chairs
near the cemetery gate. And the Pickup Artist, around
whom no one was safe. And there was Crazy Shouting
Man, owner of three ragtag mutts and an elder
statesman of the cemetery, who, when I finally talked to
him, wasn't Crazy Shouting Man at all. His name was
Al, who said, "There are loads of people up there that
I see all the time, some of them I've been seeing for
years and I don't know their name. I recognize them
and they recognize me, we talk about all sorts of things,
and it just never really occurs to you to ask their name
because you know their dog's name.

"As a matter of fact, I've always had these funny
occasions where you run into people that you talk to a
lot at the cemetery—you meet them somewhere . . . we
were down at Granny Killam's when it was open one
night and this woman came over and said, 'Al, how are
you? How're the dogs? How's all this?' and I was with a
bunch of friends and I thought, And this is . . . , and I
realized that I had no idea, it wasn't that I had forgotten her name, it was that I'd never known her name. I
knew her dog . . . I mean, I had no idea. And this was not

somebody I just knew very casually, this was somebody I probably walked with three or four mornings a week. But you always find you know a lot more dogs than you know people, which, I think, says something about who's worth knowing anyway."

Even today what strikes me as amazing about the cemetery is that there are people here, people who show up twice a day and see other people here twice a day for years, and many of them just don't know each other's real name, let alone what the other does for a living, or dream of at night, or love or hate. They just know each other's dogs' names. So when they refer to one another, they might say, "Circe's mom said Milk-Bones are full of preservatives, which is why she cooks her own." Or when they bump into each other downtown Christmas shopping, they'll say, "Ellroy's mom!" and then, when nothing's left to say, say, "Uh, how goes it?"

Was this intimacy or a complete lack of intimacy? Sometimes it felt like both at once. You had the warmth of intimacy and the comfort of hiding behind your dog. And yet every day you saw people at their most naked, talking baby-talk to their hounds, kneeling to pick up poop. I asked my friend Julie, Reuben's mother, about this.

"I think I really get a sort of window into people's . . . well, into people's souls. You watch people very content-edly walking around, throwing the ball, interacting with their dogs or totally ignoring their dogs, and going at their own pace and every once in a while yelling for their dog and . . ."

Here's Al again: "I mean, I really judge people by how they behave toward their dog. When I see people hit a dog, I'm really sort of appalled and amazed that you would do that.

"I mean, I know who really, really likes their dogs and who doesn't. I know people who've got trophy dogs and people who've got the scruffiest, ugliest dog, but they really, really love that dog."

I think it was the love part that kept me going back to the cemetery. And then it became my social hour, my escape, where, more often than not, I'd find Jeff and Keana. The minute Jeff realized I was a writer he went to the library, and over the course of a week read everything I'd ever written. And then, to my horror, wanted to talk about it. And he did this kind of thing with others, too.

When the leaves began to change during my first October in the West End Cemetery, Jeff was already talking about a Christmas card he was planning—a photograph of Keana and himself. He brought it up obsessively, about how Keana was going to have a haircut and shampoo and have her nails clipped, and how he had arranged for a photographer, and how they were scouting locations. There were ups and downs in the saga as it played out over weeks—a good location that might not work out the day of the shoot if a nor'easter hit, the need to time everything just perfectly so that Keana would leave the beauty parlor and then immediately sit for her picture before she could come back to the cemetery and get muddy.

In retrospect there were little clues even then that something strange was going on with Jeff. While he said he owned a truck, I saw him only at bus stops around town. And the scuba diving . . . later when I called various outfits in Portland, no one had ever heard of him. In the end, he had the photographs taken at Sears, he and Keana in the stiff, unsmiling pose of a Civil War—era husband and wife, he in his familiar blue sweatshirt hulking behind Keana, who was perfectly coifed. He was beaming when he handed the Christmas card to me, literally beaming.

After Christmas I left the country for several weeks and when I came back, some time after a massive icestorm, Jeff was nowhere to be found. The cemetery glittered with glazed headstones. It took days to unravel the story because people didn't seem to want to talk about it . . . didn't seem to want to talk about anything. Everyone just bundled into themselves, and Jeff . . . he was a very touchy subject, one that suddenly made us all feel defensive. What I learned was this: He'd had health problems, an infection of some kind. He went to the hospital at the same time that he was apparently forced out of his apartment. Money was tight. He'd asked someone from the cemetery to put him up, another line crossed. But that hadn't worked out. Keana was taken to a kennel by Megan, Matty's mom. And now she was calling the kennel regularly to see if Jeff had picked her up, but he hadn't. Week after week she called until it was clear that Jeff couldn't or wouldn't pick up Keana, that he was gone. That's when Keana was adopted by someone else.

Here's Megan: "You start talking about this stuff with somebody and then you realize, I didn't even know this person . . . like with Jeff, I mean, it was like you knew everything about his life but in the end how much of that was actually true? And, you know, you didn't even know this person . . . it was like August to December and he was gone. But it seemed like forever."

There were completely unsubstantiated rumors that he'd robbed a bank. Someone knew someone whose cousin had seen his photo on a Boston newscast. Maybe. But then most people were quick to accept this as fact. In a weird way, I wonder if we felt betrayed. Betrayed because Jeff had broken the simple rules of the cemetery. He'd become too intimate. Now he was gone and it was hard to say hi, let alone catch someone else's eye. During those dark winter months the cemetery became a kind of haunted, trustless place. In one of those endless conversations we had about him later, some people worried that he knew where we lived . . . someone threatened to track him down. But what for? So that he might never again bamboozle other hapless dog owners in other seaside towns into chatting about doggy shampoo?

Sara and I kept the Christmas card on our refrigerator right up until a couple of months ago, actually, when it quietly fell to a new rotation of refrigerator photos. We kept it there in hopes, I think, that he would come back and explain where he'd been, for I was pretty certain that he couldn't have robbed a bank. And if he had, I told myself, maybe it was because he had to. Maybe he'd been inches from a life he imagined for himself, with a dog that gave unconditional love, with friends he was guaranteed to see every day and he'd had a couple of bad breaks—got sick, ran out of money, lost his dog, and then panicked.

Now time has passed. People come and go and every six months the galaxy inside these gates breaks apart and reconfigures. Dogs die, people leave for nursing homes, others move, more arrive, and every day, today even, people are here walking in special circles like they're in Mecca. Circling the Kaaba. In general I'd say things are back to the way they were—intimate but not intimate. We stand around in dumfounded joy with ten, twenty, thirty other gaping down adults, reveling in the simplicity of stupidly entertaining dog play. Dalmatian Man still flashes sign language at his deaf Dalmatian, the Pickup Artist still works his magic, the Lawn Chair Family still sets up by the cemetery gate each day, covering their legs with wool blankets.

Fact is, even without somebody like Jeff pulling people together, if you stand on a corner with a bunch of strangers, eventually something happens that brings you together. Sometimes something small. The other night I went to the cemetery at sunset. There were the same broken headstones, the same sea captains and paupers, and there were all these living people, too, who only knew me as Trout's dad, or as the guy who stupidly named his dog Trout, or however they see me. The dogs were playing hard, racing in circles, not wanting any of it to end, and a gigantic moon came up, came up tangerine. It was the kind of moon that stills everything, and we stood in a circle watching it rise. For a minute or two we just stood there glowing orange; the dogs didn't exist at all.

Christmases
from *My Dog Skip*

WILLIE MORRIS

*W*e loved the town at Christmas, in the clear, cool air, the lights aglitter in front of the established houses on the hills and down in the flat places, the sudden containment and luster. Skip would accompany our church group as we went caroling, and as we observed the heavenly path of the star, it must have been *the* star, as it moved across the skies from around Belzoni out in the Delta, up over Brickyard Hill and Peak Tenereffe; snug on such a night, the Christmas carols were the most peaceful blessings in all the world. Our friends and I and Skip would take Christmas baskets to poor people living in shabby little cabins in the hills and feel glad that our families were not in such bad straits.

Rivers Applewhite, Skip, and I had a custom on Christmas Eve of walking down Main Street to look at the bustling crowds and the decorations, then out into the residential sections to see the Christmas trees in the windows. The town seemed expectant, all laid out and still under the pristine December night.

A few days before one Christmas it snowed: this was for us a most rare and majestic event. I had seen snow once before, when I was very small, but most of the younger children never had, and they went wild with joy. Skip had never seen snow either, and I observed him as he pranced in it on our lawn, rolled about in it, and tried to catch the flakes in his mouth. I went a little berserk myself and started shooting baskets in the backyard in it, enjoying the sound of a successful shot made through the frozen basketball net. The next day Skip and I trudged to the top of Brickyard Hill with a sled. He sat in front of me and I held him tightly as we descended in an exuberant swoop all the way down to the cemetery. We did it again and again, returning home exhausted from the countless treks to the apex of the hill. That snow, if you can believe it, lasted on the ground for four days, and the old townspeople still remember it with reverence.

Christmas mornings were warm with the familiar ritual. We would wake up shortly after dawn in our house—my father, my mother, Skip and I. Skip would have aroused me out of sleep with his nose as always, then bitten my toes, then pulled the blankets off me with his teeth to make sure I would not tarry any longer. No worry about that on *this* day. We would open the presents, and Skip would have his own stocking: a new tennis ball in it, perhaps, and a package of bologna and fried chicken livers, and a new collar. My mother would play three or four carols on the baby grand; then we would have the sparsest of breakfasts to save room for the feast to come.

Under the purple clouds we would drive the forty miles south to Jackson to be with my grandmother Mamie, my grandfather Percy, and my incorrigible great-aunts Maggie and Susie. The drive itself is etched in memory, the same we took the night Skip was ill—the tossing hills and the frost on the ground and the tiny hamlets on the plain with their wan, lost facades where children played outside with their acquisitions of the day, and finally the splendid glimpse of the Capitol dome and the ride down State Street to the little brick house on North Jefferson. When Skip saw the familiar house he would bound out of the car swift as a fox, and I was not far behind.

They would be there on the gallery under the magnolia trees waiting for us, the four of them, and we would all go inside to exultant embracings to exchange our gifts, modest items for sure, and examine what we had given one another. Once Skip got a rubber mouse that squeaked, and proceeded to bite it in two. And the smells from the kitchen! The fat turkey and giblet gravy and cornbread stuffing and sweet potatoes with melted marshmallows and the orange nectar and ambrosia and roasted pecans and mincemeat pies! Skip hovered around the oven while nibbling on a roasted pecan and my two great-aunts, who could not see very well, bumped into each other every now and again and wished each other Merry Christmas, while the rest of us sank into the chairs by the fire in the parlor and awaited what my grandmother was making for us. Christmas songs wafted from the chimes of the church down the way, and the crackle of firecrackers came from the neighboring lawns, and my grandmother would dart out of the kitchen with Skip at her heels and say, "Almost done now!"

Then, at eleven in the morning, never later, we would sit at the ancient table, which had been my great-great-grandmother's; my grandfather Percy and my father at opposite ends, my mother and great-aunts on one side of it, my grandmother and I on the other, Old Skip poised next to my chair, expecting his favors. Occasionally I would slip him a turkey gizzard or liver or wing. We sat there for two hours, it seemed, prattling about many things. The clock on the mantel would sound every quarter-hour, and my great-aunts would ask for more servings and say, "My, ain't this *good*?" I would look around every year at each of them, and feel Skip's nose on my hand, and listen to the talk, as if all this was designed for the two of us alone. Then, after the rattling of dishes, and after Skip had dined on leftover dressing and pieces of turkey, we would settle in the parlor again, drowsy and fulfilled, Skip stretching out on the carpet in his Yuletide torpor. Finally my grandmother, standing before us by the fire, would gaze about the room and always say, in her tone at once tender and bemused: "Oh well, another Christmas come and gone."

Mel's Story

MATTHEW "UNCLE MATTY" MARGOLIS

Who would have known that such a little bundle of fur could bring so much joy to our lives? I have been in the dog training business for thirty-eight years and have personally had many dogs in my lifetime. You can document the history of your life by your animals, and they are all special in their own way. However, sometimes there is a dog that just touches you as no other has. I met my wife through her little Cardigan corgi, Pebbles, and my life changed in the most wonderful way. This was my first experience living with a corgi and that was all it took. Someone told me once that corgis are like potato chips—just can't have one. And he was right. Even though we already had a beautiful shepherd named Idol, we decided to get a second Cardigan corgi. The search was on.

Mel was a Blue Merle Cardigan Welsh corgi with one brown eye and one blue eye. He was the first dog that my wife and I picked out together. We flew to Pennsylvania to pick him up and he was just the cutest little thing. Being the dog trainer that I am, I did all of the testing on him and we both fell in love immediately.

He was such a happy little puppy and always full of fun. My wife, Rose, did most of the training and I supervised. On one occasion, Rose said to me "I think he's ready to sleep in the bedroom with the other dogs and not in his crate." I explained to her that he was still quite young and not ready for freedom yet. Well, she persuaded me in her loving way to give it a try. We went to sleep that night, and the next morning, discovered that the bottom drawer of our antique armoire was newly decorated. Little Mel had chewed his way to the inside. Uncle Matty to the rescue! We had the drawer repaired and Mel was sleeping in his crate once again (where he was the happiest anyway).

Mel was a real social animal. He loved people and other animals, never barked or chased the birds, squirrels, deer, or other critters that were always strolling through our property. Mel would sit and look at our miniature donkeys . . . and it wasn't long before he and one of the donkeys, Rex, became fast friends. They would kiss each other on the noses through the fence. Mel was, indeed, enriching the lives of all of us.

He was in heaven at agility classes, where he excelled. In fact, every time we took him to an event as a spectator, he barked like crazy and wanted to participate. He traveled everywhere with us and one time, Rose said to me, "Matty, I think Mel might be ready to ride in the car with the other dogs and not in his crate—what do you think?" Well, you can guess my response. She lovingly persuaded me once again and well—he ate the leather seat. This time, though, I had to travel to give a dog training lesson. We brought along all three dogs and drove up to the clients' house. When we were finished with the lesson, the owners walked us out to our car and saw the seat. They asked what happened and my wife explained about Mel. Needless to say, this was not very good advertising for a dog trainer.

We had so many adventures with little Mel, and he brought so much joy to our lives. He was a clown when playing with us or the other dogs. He loved being in the limelight and Rose would call him her "goofy kid." They had developed a special bond. Mel was always her shadow and Rose wouldn't have it any other way.

This past December, we noticed that he was not feeling

well and took him to the veterinarian. We all thought he just had an upset stomach, but he kept getting worse and worse. We brought him to a specialist and discovered that at the young age of four years old, he had cancer and it was incurable. He only had a few more days to live. We were devastated. He was too young to be so sick. But he was, and he soon passed on to the Rainbow Bridge. I believe he looks down upon us and all his many friends.

As I've said before, you can document your life by the animals that have shared it with you. They are all special. Yet sometimes there is that one dog that penetrates your heart like no other. That was Mel. He taught me a lot. His joy made me happier. His sweetness taught me patience. His humor made me laugh. His love of every living thing emphasized tolerance. His death made me appreciate life even more. And even though we miss him, we know he is alive in our hearts.

But like the man said, "You can't have just one." We recently welcomed little Barney, another Blue Merle Cardigan corgi into our lives. He is different in every way from Mel and a joy unto his own. And just in case you were wondering, he is still sleeping in his crate and will not be riding fancy-free in the SUV anytime soon.

Christmas Memories
from *Southern Fried Divorce*

JUDY CONNER

*N*ot long after I became his ex-wife, that ex-husband brought me a .38 blue steel revolver and a brown fuzzy puppy. His unannounced arrival at my new bachelorette maisonette was not a complete surprise. He'd always been fond of barging in where not invited. So I didn't really expect him to stand on ceremony and wait for an invitation that might be delayed indefinitely.

I barely heard the doorbell over the sound of the Carrollton Avenue streetcar as it passed, headed for the nearby car barn to be watered and fed. I opened the door of my shotgun double apartment to greet my former mate, beaming with goodwill and Jim Beam. He was festooned with red and green ribbon and carrying a couple of intriguing items. Belated Christmas offerings, I guessed, since we were pretty deep into spring.

"Surprise!" he bellowed. "And seasonable greetings! Here, I've brought you a new home security package. You can learn how to shoot this gun and this puppy'll grow up to be a fine watchdog. Lookit how he's watching you right now."

"Well, how thoughtful," I murmured.

After his fifteen years of quasi-husbanding, I guess he was finding it hard to quit at least musing on my welfare. Crime in New Orleans at the time was common as mildew. Just part of the landscape. One of the downsides to the endearing openness of the locals is that they might open your door as readily as they open their own. What's yours is theirs. They just don't have well-defined boundaries.

I toyed with five bullets that accompanied the gun and wondered what kind of fool gives his ex-wife a gun. Especially one who sometimes has the disposition of a wolverine. And why'd he get only five bullets for a six-shooter? Perhaps for a game of Redneck roulette? It's similar to Russian roulette, just a whole lot more daring. Your average redneck will rarely resist a dare. That probably helps account for their historically out-of-proportion representation in the wartime military. They've always figured prominently in the body counts too.

For Russian roulette, they use one bullet and five empty chambers—because of the Russian economy. Shortages of everything but vodka, so I hear. The redneck version is just the reverse—five bullets, one empty chamber. Much more efficient. Anyhow, a gun was not something I'd have chosen for myself. However, I didn't already have one and this one appeared to be a nice, sturdy model and not at all cheap. It's the thought that counts.

"What made you think to get me a dog?" I asked him.

Now that ex-husband got all fired up. "It was just pitiful," he said. "I was over by Franky and Johnny's picking up some hot crawfish when I saw a bunch of kids there on Tchoupitoulas Street. When I drove closer, I saw that they had a hold of this puppy's arms and legs. They were teasing him and pulling on him. I just whipped my car off to the side and jumped out and started hollering and slinging kids. I snatched this puppy up and took off. As I was driving along, of course, I thought of you and how you just love puppies."

It was, of course, true that I love puppies. And pie. And Mother and the flag. And assorted strays of all kinds.

My glance shifted from the puppy to the broad, usually guileless face of that ex-husband. The innocent look was gone, replaced by that other one. He lied about stuff to save his hide. He was a sport-liar and a real enthusiast of writer Dan Jenkins' "Are you going to believe me or your lyin' eyes?" And to a lesser degree, "That's my story and I'm stickin' to it!"

"What's the real deal on the dog?" I snapped.

"Well I was over at Joey K's eating a shrimp po'boy with Clay. You know Clay is the guy who bought Joey K's from Joey K."

"Yes, I know that, I go there all the time. What does that have to do with this dog?" I wondered if very many people lie about their lunch.

"Joey K was in there too, eating a po'boy with Clay. And having a beer in one of those big ole heavy iced-tea glasses Clay uses. Joey K's brown dog, Betty, was there, and her puppies—just the right size for giving away. As you can see," he answered.

I could see a light-brown fuzz ball about the size of a cantaloupe with dark eyes and nose and eyebrows. Mighty cute. How many ugly puppies have you seen? I'm pretty sure there are way more ugly babies. If this one took after his mother, Betty, he'd grow up to be a medium-brown, medium-hound-type dog. Generic dog. But the eyebrows were a redeeming factor. I purely love a dog with eyebrows.

So, I bedded the critter down in the laundry room at the very back of the shotgun—as far from the bedrooms as possible. I was hoping that the pup would let me and my new housemate get some sleep.

I had lately opened my heart and my hearth to that ex-husband's nephew. I could not do otherwise. Whenever I got ready to fly that ex-husband's coop, that nephew said, "You're not going off and leaving me here by myself with my crazy uncle." I didn't mind. I was used to the teenager. He'd been with us for several years—ever since his mother had run off and joined the circus or the itinerant preachers or something. I forget. But the nephew was pretty different from both his mother and his uncle, who acted like they'd been raised by wild dogs. He was just as sweet and smart and talented as could be. He showed a very early flair for the dramatic. During a visit to our house, he came into my bedroom as I was blabbing away on the phone. Three-year-olds can't stand for you to get on the phone or in the bathtub. I was barely aware of him there at the foot of the bed. I focused a bit and saw that he was gesturing mightily with three fingers of his right hand and madly raising his baby eyebrows up and down. "Three?" I mouthed at him. He nodded vigorously and began wildly bobbing and weaving. Then he raised his left hand behind him, lunged toward me flapping his right foot on the floor, and pointed his right hand in a brilliant feint á la Errol Flynn. Abruptly, he stopped and again was stabbing the air with the three fingers. I got it, I got it! He wanted one of the Three Musketeers candy bars I'd squirreled away in the kitchen. Hiding things up high never worked; he could climb anything. But he never thought to stick his grimy paw into the canister of dried red beans sitting innocently on the counter. I ended my phone call and gave his charade my full attention. He got a hearty "Bravo" and the candy bar.

Really, the only way he was like his family was that he was mighty messy. All them people were like pigs. We had an agreement whereby he'd keep his mess hemmed up in his room. So the common areas looked pretty good.

We had plenty of stuff because I had taken most of the furniture and every last knickknack. I think I left that ex-husband the king-sized bed, the TV, the refrigerator, and an easy chair. To his credit, he had insisted that I take everything.

I wasn't too sure about this new puppy business. My confidence in my housebreaking abilities had been badly shaken by the failure of my marriage. I had put just about every scrap of energy I could muster into getting that husband to behave—with virtually no effect. Impervious. Based on my recent track record, I guessed I'd very shortly be knee-deep in puppy-poop. Although I guess if I wanted to, I could claim success at keeping that ex-husband from shitting on the floor. Of course, in a couple of weeks, my laundry room looked like the launching area for a school paper drive—lots and lots of nice clean newspaper. Not so the floor. That puppy had carefully, precisely shat betwixt the sheets of paper. I had scooped about four or five hundred piles of puppy poop off the floor and was past ready to quit.

I rang up that ex-husband and I said, "I love my new gun, but I'm fixing to take this brown dog to the pound."

Naturally, he came thundering over to intervene on the dog's behalf and call me names. "This is just plain heartless! You are the meanest woman in the world," he declared. "Not to mention ungrateful. This was a Christmas present!"

"Oh, it was not either. You just wanted to show off.

And since you're so crazy about being the big hero, you can *just rescue this!*"

"I don't have *time* for a puppy."

"I don't either, but I do have time to take him to the ASPCA!"

"Well, dammit!" he countered brilliantly.

"Yeah, dammit all," I declared. "You've got yourself a new brown dog!"

In fact, I had really done that ex-husband a favor. His nightclub business left his days pretty flexible. He could really use somebody to hang with since he was even harder on buddies that he was on wives. Just ask the one who had two loads of river sand show up on his front lawn. Just ask the one who got his picture taken—nekkid and tied to a bedstead by some slut in that ex-husband's "office." Just ask any one of a dozen or so who happened to be standing next to him when he took a notion to taunt bikers, seamen, drug dealers, or other assorted thugs. And just ask the one who got tricked into carrying that ex-husband's bag through customs when they returned from a trip to Thailand. Yep, ask the guy how he felt when the inspector popped it open and found nothing but pills, tablets, and capsules—thousands of them, just look in there, full to the brim. It looked like somebody'd spent their entire vacation filling a suitcase with M&M's.

A puppy was just the kind of companion that ex-husband needed. The two became immediately inseparable. They'd set out together just about every day. They'd go to the hardware store and to the bank and to his nightclub business to harass the employees. He was in charge of the human resources part of the business. He also booked the nightly live music and took care of the endless bunch of crap that came with owning a club. Or any small business, for that matter. The advertising and marketing were my areas of expertise. After we split up, we continued the business partnership as before, except that I also started booking the music. I didn't want to but it was the only way I could get that ex-husband to readily agree to my full financial support. The real story was that he was damn sick and tired of booking music. He was always angling to do less of anything that did not directly pertain to plumbing or chasing nasty women. That man loved a broken or plugged-up toilet better than anything—even the nasty women. We had once talked about his becoming a plumber. My position was one of neutrality, but I had pointed out that it would be a shame for him to drop out of law school to become a plumber unless he was really committed to his vocation.

As it turned out, he was not really committed to pipes and drains and hair balls and such. It was just that he had discovered that he was uncommitted to and bored blind by the law. The study of it, that is. He had always had an aversion to obeying it. I believe he may still hold the record for "drunk and disorderlies" in his home area—the northwest section of the District of Columbia.

One fine day in New Orleans, he was yet again not in class. He wandered into a neighborhood bar on Lowerline Street. It was called the University Inn because it was near Tulane University. He fell in love with the place. Pretty soon he had convinced the owner, Bob, that a partner would be just the thing. Poor Bob. As soon as he could thereafter, he bought Bob out. Thus began his professional career in adult recreation. We both assumed that his extensive experience as an amateur would stand him in good stead.

We offered only draft beer, peanuts, and hilarity for a clientele consisting mostly of the neighborhood rabble plus Tulane students and faculty. But for such a hole-in-the-wall, it did well. And it was big fun. It was mighty convenient for that ex-husband. He had found an occupation where he could pretty much be a shiftless ne'er-do-well right there on the job.

Just about the time his lease on the space was running out, he had saved up some money. With the help of one of his faithful customers, Matt Gregory, he was able to buy a building and open a new and improved fun spot.

Matt was the first native New Orleanian who was willing to be our friend. And it took us two years to get him. As a matter of fact, I was wondering if we'd ever get one. It was so weird because I'd been pretty popular in college and that ex-husband had always had a bunch of friends, albethey motley. We even discussed the possibility that we might, in fact, be a pair of losers. What if, during those years of prancing around all biggety-speckle, thinking we were mighty cute and pretty cool, we were actually kinda creepy? But no, that couldn't be it.

We finally did figure out why it was so hard to make friends among the natives. It's because most of the people who are born here never leave and if they do they spend the rest of their lives trying to get back. And most of 'em are Catholic, tending to larger families. So everyone you meet has friends going back to kindergarten plus cousins ahoy. In fact, right from the start, children are encouraged to be best friends with their cousins. Isn't that strange? It's like they're all in the Mafia or something. Even when they give big parties, their guest lists are just about filled up with family. These folks do not get to do hardly anything without the whole damn family. They just plain don't have time in their lives for anybody new. You've just got to be real patient till they can fit you in. It is true, though, that once they do make a place for you in their lives, it's pretty hard to get yourself kicked out.

For instance—Matt Gregory—guess what we did to him? I have to say "we" because this was one of the few times where I was involved in some nefarious activity with that ex-husband. At the time, Matt was married to his first wife. He was also carrying on an extramarital affair of which we did not approve. Naturally, I didn't approve, but I thought it pretty fascinating that that ex-husband didn't either. Even I knew this was a really black pot calling names. Fairness notwithstanding, that ex-husband was extremely vocal in his criticism of Matt and his "Nymphet," as we had christened the hapless honey. He even barred the twosome from the tavern. Although Matt was welcomed solo. There came the time that we knew in advance that Matt would be out of town. He was going to New York for a week on business. He had been foolish enough to divulge that the "Nymphet" would be meeting him there. This plan really annoyed that ex-husband and he ranted about it quite a bit. We kicked it around and finally, between us, developed a plan. We wrote a press release for a newspaper column dedicated to the doings of locals. We sent it in and it was printed.

Attorney Matt Gregory will be jetting to New York

for the KNOBGLOBBEN SUGAR FESTIVAL

and will be enjoying same for the better part

of next week.

Oh, by the way, "Sugar" was the nymphet's name.

That ex-husband was kind enough to warn him that something might be in the paper sometime. Poor Matt had to get up at dawn: five-thirty every day for weeks to snag the paper before his wife got up.

Now, even after that, Matt helped us purchase the property that would house the next bigger and better nightclub.

The new establishment was located on Oak Street, in the heart of the Carrollton area. The Mardi Gras parade put on by the Krewe of Carrollton used to roll on Oak Street. The route was changed because one year there was a real high wind that blew a krewe member off the float when it was on an overpass. It was very bad. The new plan excluded Oak Street. I think that marked the beginning of the street's eventual decline as a center of commerce.

The brown dog and that ex-husband spent so much time together that after a while there came to be a family resemblance between them. I once remarked to that ex-husband that the brown dog looked quite a bit like his cousin—one of the ones who'd run off to join the circus or pick fruit or something. I forget. She had a long, thin brown face and brown eyes. Just like the brown dog. That ex-husband's face was brown year round also and he had the brown eyes. But he had a very big face. Taking up more than fifty percent of his head and kind of squarish. So he and the dog didn't look so much alike except through the eyes. That ex-husband replied snappishly that the dog was still a teenager and would surely outgrow the resemblance to the cousin.

Very big faces run in my family too. Along with some

pretty big butts. Big tits do not run in my family. However, I was blessed as a mutant in that department. I can assure you that big tits never go out of style. If we could just get it where big butts are popular, life would be perfect.

I guess the brown dog had been with that ex-husband about a year when I began the custom of the Christmas roast. I fixed it the same way every year and the brown dog liked it very, very much. It went thus:

Take a 5- or 6-pound roast—I would choose a sirloin tip, but you could use a cheaper cut if you're the stingy type. In my own case, it's pretty much "Nothin's too good for this dog."

Preheat oven to 500°F—yep, that's 500°. Hot. Mix together 4 teaspoons of salt, 2 teaspoons of cayenne pepper, 2 teaspoons of coarse ground black pepper. Smear this mixture all over the roast. Cook uncovered in a Dutch oven or big iron skillet for 7 minutes per pound. Turn the oven off and DO NOT OPEN THE OVEN DOOR. Do not open the door right from the start and not for at least an hour and a half after you turn the oven off. You will be tempted to peep in and out of there, but DON'T DO IT—it will mess it up if you do. If you cannot follow these directions, cook your roast some other way. When the time is up, remove and let stand for 10 minutes.

For people: slice and serve. For brown dogs: cut off the spicy crust. This roast will be rare. You can cook longer per pound if your dog prefers medium or well-done.

When I fix this roast for people, I also make these killer mashed potatoes—even though there will not be a whole lot of gravy.

White or red taters will do. Peel, slice, cover with water in pretty heavy pot. Bring to a boil, then simmer till done. Drain in colander and dump taters back in the pot. Add lots of butter, some salt, and white pepper to taste. Do not substitute black pepper—it's not the same. Pour in a dab of whipping cream and mash it all together. Then whisk, adding cream as needed, till you get the texture you like. I like some lumps myself. Good as ice cream.

The brown dog would come to sleep over at my house so he'd have time to eat all of the roast. It was hard, but he persevered. I'd serve him the first portion for early dinner, around five in the afternoon. He'd feed intermittently throughout the evening and finish up about two a.m. Then he would go fast asleep with all four legs straight up in the air, which would soon be thick with brown-dog gas. Sometimes he'd fart so loud that he'd wake himself up. Then he would look around suspiciously, growling softly for good measure. He'd give a big yawn—tasting it—smack, smack, smack, and nod back off.

The reason I cooked a whole roast for the brown dog was, even though I'd given him to that ex-husband, I wanted the dog to like me best. It was a common desire of mine. I might not be the only one, but I would, by God, be number one.

I am pleased to report that my Christmas roast was his favorite present, and the brown dog looked forward to the consumption with glee. You could readily tell this because the only time he broke out of a shuffle was from the car to my front door for that Christmas roast. He generally liked to move as slowly as possible to annoy that ex-husband. The brown dog would usually stall around in the car, yawning and stretching, until he'd been invited to disembark at least three or four times. And even then he'd move like a thousand-year-old dog. Well, on Christmas Roast Night, he'd bound from that car before it was stopped good, and his nails on the sidewalk would be shootin' sparks. You're probably wondering how he knew Roast Night from any other. Well, he was always a great one for skulking around and eavesdropping. Sometimes I would manage to surprise him. I'd phone up that ex-husband and tell him, "Now don't say anything, just listen. I don't want the brown dog to know, so bring him over for the roast two days before Christmas."

One time that ex-husband brought along a friend, besides the brown dog, for the roast. It was this guy from Ireland who, by the way, was on a list of the ten most eligible bachelors in all of Ireland. Since he had this actual credential, I was, at first, pleased when he pronounced me a winsome lass, even though I was pretty sure that the top scorer would be the toothsome wench. This was a most charming Irishman, but his general attitude regarding the consumption of spirits and, well, work would clearly make him ineligible for any list of marriageable guys that I would compile. I think that country might have had more problems than bad food, bad teeth, and a history of crop failure. I think it is so great that the Irish have turned their country around so nicely.

Mr. Ireland was not my only foreign encounter that day. Earlier, I'd been to a holiday reception at the International Trade Mart. I was greeted by a very charming Latin gentleman. He smiled, bowed slightly over my hand, and said, "Feliz Navidad." I replied happily, "So nice to meet you, Feliz." After meeting half a dozen or so fun-seekers, all named Feliz, I figured it out: "Feliz" is Spanish for "dude."

Anyway, that ex-husband and his Irish buddy decided to stay for the consumption. They were shortly joined by that ex-husband's nephew, who loved celebrations of all kinds ever since his mother had run off with the circus or the tinkers. I forget which. Warm greetings were exchanged all around and I handed out bourbons, which is what we drank in the winter. Everyone gathered at my big round kitchen table to be near the ice and await the appearance of the roast. I had comfy chairs and lots and lots of red doodads in my kitchen, so it was hard to keep folks out of there. In no time, we were all aglow from the bourbon and that really hot oven.

"We had a r-r-really interrrresting time, last night," the Irishman offered in his Irish whiskey burr-voice.

"Oh, yeah," I mumbled, as I glared at that ex-husband, since they'd had that nephew out with them.

"*Yeah*," the nephew chimed in excitedly. "I got to play piano with Jimmy Buffet. He came in the club last night and we all went out later. We stopped by the bar at the Pontchartrain Hotel and they let us noodle around on the piano. It was great!" This was exciting stuff for that nephew, and for us all, really. We'd always been Parrotheads. Partly because Fingers Taylor, Buffet's best harp player, is from Mississippi, like me, and an old friend. Of course, Buffet's from Hattiesburg originally. That Mississippi deal is always there.

A week or so later, the story of the Nephew/Buffet piano duet was written up in the *Times-Picayune* newspaper. And neither me nor that ex-husband was responsible for it being in the paper. A lot of folks saw it and it was big fun.

I provided another round of bourbons, and the three guys began to feel peckish just as the roast had ripened. They were clamoring for shares in the brown dog's roast and snatching the slices as quickly as they slid from my knife. The brown dog's eyes were darting back and forth nervously from the roast to their mouths. He had yet to receive the first taste. What started as a whine of entreaty became snarls of indignation. That dog knew what was fair, and this was not it. He maneuvered himself between them and the roast and would not give way. They knew they'd been bested, and were obliged to settle for some impromptu nabs. Historically speaking, Nabs were little packs of crackers put out by Nabisco and sold in little grocery stores and service stations throughout the rural South. But if it's me talking, then nabs are anything eaten between meals. In this case it happened to be some honey-baked ham, ready-made from a ham store. I had, by the way, invested more time in acquiring that ham than I spend with some members of my family. During the holidays, those ham stores are like a box full of monkeys. They have to have some ham cops on duty to get to the head of the line, which snakes around through those brass poles and velvet ropes. Like at the bank, for crying out loud. "I'd like to withdraw a five-to-seven-pound spiral-sliced ham, please, ma'am."

I served the brown dog a very large helping of Christmas roast, with the spicy crust off. The guys eagerly snarfed the brown dog's leavings. I took my place at the table to enjoy the Ezra Brooks fifteen-year-old. This was some of the best sipping whiskey there ever was, but don't go looking for it. They quit making it. Come December, I remember it fondly as I do the look on that little hound face every year when the brown dog would first lay eyes on his Christmas roast.

Tricki Woo

from *James Herriot's Dog Stories*

JAMES HERRIOT

As autumn wore into winter and the high tops were streaked with the first snows, the discomforts of practice in the Dales began to make themselves felt.

Driving for hours with frozen feet, climbing to the high barns in biting winds which seared and flattened the wiry hill grass; the interminable stripping off in draughty buildings and the washing of hands and chests in buckets of cold water, using scrubbing soap and often a piece of sacking for a towel.

I really found out the meaning of chapped hands. When there was a rush of work, my hands were never quite dry, and the little red fissures crept up almost to my elbows.

This was when some small animal work came as a blessed relief. To step out of the rough, hard routine for a while; to walk into a warm drawing-room instead of a cow house and tackle something less formidable than a horse or a bull. And among all those comfortable drawing-rooms there was none so beguiling as Mrs. Pumphrey's.

Mrs. Pumphrey was an elderly widow. Her late husband, a beer baron whose breweries and pubs were scattered widely over the broad bosom of Yorkshire, had left her a vast fortune and a beautiful house on the outskirts of Darrowby. Here she lived with a large staff of servants, a gardener, a chauffeur, and Tricki Woo. Tricki Woo was a Pekingese and the apple of his mistress's eye.

Standing now in the magnificent doorway, I furtively rubbed the toes of my shoes on the backs of my trousers and blew on my cold hands. I could almost see the deep armchair drawn close to the leaping flames, the tray of cocktail biscuits, the bottle of excellent sherry. Because of the sherry, I was always careful to time my visits for half an hour before lunch.

A maid answered my ring, beaming on me as an honoured guest, and led me to the room, crammed with expensive furniture and littered with glossy magazines and the latest novels. Mrs. Pumphrey, in the high-backed chair by the fire, put down her book with a cry of delight. "Trick! Trick! Here is your uncle Herriot." I had been made an uncle very early and, sensing the advantages of the relationship, had made no objection.

Tricki, as always, bounded from his cushion, leaped on to the back of the sofa and put his paws on my shoulders. He then licked my face thoroughly before retiring, exhausted. He was soon exhausted because he was given roughly twice the amount of food needed for a dog of his size. And it was the wrong kind of food.

"Oh, Mr. Herriot," Mrs. Pumphrey said, looking at her pet anxiously. "I'm so glad you've come. Tricki has gone flop-bott again."

This ailment, not to be found in any text book, was her way of describing the symptoms of Tricki's impacted anal glands. When the glands filled up, he showed discomfort by sitting down suddenly in mid-walk and his mistress would rush to the phone in great agitation.

"Mr. Herriot! Please come, he's gone flop-bott again!"

I hoisted the little dog onto a table and, by pressure on

the anus with a pad of cotton wool, I evacuated the glands.

It baffled me that the Peke was always so glad to see me. Any dog who could still like a man who grabbed him and squeezed his bottom hard every time they met had to have an incredibly forgiving nature. But Tricki never showed any resentment; in fact he was an outstandingly equable little animal, bursting with intelligence, and I was genuinely attached to him. It was a pleasure to be his personal physician.

The squeezing over, I lifted my patient from the table, noticing the increased weight, the padding of extra flesh over the ribs. "You know, Mrs. Pumphrey, you're overfeeding him again. Didn't I tell you to cut out all those pieces of cake and give him more protein?"

"Oh yes, Mr. Herriot," Mrs. Pumphrey wailed. "But what can I do? He's so tired of chicken."

I shrugged; it was hopeless. I allowed the maid to lead me to the palatial bathroom where I always performed a ritual handwashing after the operation. It was a huge room with a fully stocked dressing table, massive green ware and rows of glass shelves laden with toilet preparations. My private guest towel was laid out next to the slab of expensive soap.

Then I returned to the drawing-room, my sherry glass was filled, and I settled down by the fire to listen to Mrs. Pumphrey. It couldn't be called a conversation, because she did all the talking, but I always found it rewarding.

Mrs. Pumphrey was likeable, gave wildly to charities and would help anyone in trouble. She was intelligent and amusing and had a lot of waffling charm; but most people have a blind spot and hers was Tricki Woo. The tales she told about her darling ranged far into the realms of fantasy, and I waited eagerly for the next installment.

"Oh Mr. Herriot, I have the most exciting news. Tricki has a pen pal! Yes, he wrote a letter to the editor of *Doggy World* enclosing a donation, and told him that even though he was descended from a long line of Chinese emperors, he had decided to come down and mingle freely with the common dogs. He asked the editor to seek out a pen pal for him among the dogs he knew so that they could correspond to their mutual benefit. And for this purpose, Tricki said he would adopt the name of Mr. Utterbunkum. And, do you know, he received the most beautiful letter from the editor" (I could imagine the sensible man leaping upon this potential goldmine) "who said he would like to introduce Bonzo Fotheringham, a lonely Dalmatian who would be delighted to exchange letters with a new friend in Yorkshire."

I sipped the sherry. Tricki snored on my lap. Mrs. Pumphrey went on.

"But I'm so disappointed about the new summer-house—you know I got it specifically for Tricki so we could sit out together on warm afternoons. It's such a nice little rustic shelter, but he's taken a passionate dislike to it. Simply loathes it—absolutely refuses to go inside. You should see the dreadful expression on his face when he looks at it. And do you know what he called it yesterday? Oh, I hardly dare tell you." She looked around the room before leaning over and whispering: "He called it 'the bloody hut'!"

The maid struck fresh life into the fire and refilled my glass. The wind hurled a handful of sleet against the window. This, I thought, was the life. I listened for more.

"And did I tell you, Mr. Herriot, Tricki had another good win yesterday? You know, I'm sure he must study the racing columns, he's such a tremendous judge of form. Well, he told me to back Canny Lad in the three o'clock at Redcar yesterday and, as usual, it won. He put on a shilling each way and got back nine shillings."

These bets were always placed in the name of Tricki Woo and I thought with compassion of the reactions of the local bookies. The Darrowby turf accountants were a harassed and fugitive body of men. A board would appear at the end of some alley urging the population to invest with Joe Downs and enjoy perfect security. Joe would live for a few months on a knife edge while he pitted his wits against knowledgeable citizens, but the end was always the same: a few favourites would win in a row and Joe would be gone in the night, taking his board with him. Once I asked a local inhabitant about the sudden departure of one of these luckless nomads. He replied unemotionally: "Oh, we brok'im."

Losing a regular flow of shillings to a dog must have been a heavy cross for these unfortunate men to bear.

"I had such a frightening experience last week," Mrs. Pumphrey continued. "I was sure I would have to call you out. Poor little Tricki—he went completely crackerdog!"

I mentally lined this up with flop-bott among the new canine diseases and asked for more information.

"It was awful. I was terrified. The gardener was throwing rings for Tricki—you know he does this for half an hour every day." Hodgkin, a dour, bent old Yorkshireman who looked as though he hated all dogs and Tricki in particular, had to go out on the lawn every day and throw little rubber rings over and over again. Tricki bounded after them and brought them back, barking madly till the process was repeated. The bitter lines on the old man's face deepened as the game progressed. His lips moved continually, but it was impossible to hear what he was saying.

Mrs. Pumphrey went on: "Well, he was playing his game, and he does adore it so, when suddenly, without warning, he went crackerdog. He forgot all about his rings and began to run around in circles, barking and yelping in such a strange way. Then he fell over on his side and lay like a little dead thing. Do you know, Mr. Herriot, I really thought he was dead, he lay so perfectly still. And what hurt me most was that Hodgkin began to laugh. He has been with me for twenty-four years and I have never even seen him smile, and yet, when he looked down at that still form, he broke into a queer, high-pitched cackle. It was horrid. I was just going to rush to the telephone when Tricki got up and walked away—he seemed perfectly normal."

Hysteria, I thought, brought on by wrong feeding and overexcitement. I put down my glass and fixed Mrs.

Pumphrey with a severe glare. "Now look, this is just what I was talking about. If you persist in feeding all that fancy rubbish to Tricki you are going to ruin his health. You really must get him on to a sensible dog diet of one or, at the most, two small meals a day of meat and brown bread or a little biscuit. And nothing in between."

Mrs. Pumphrey shrank into her chair, a picture of abject guilt. "Oh, please don't speak to me like that. I do try to give him the right things, but it is so difficult. When he begs for his little tidbits, I can't refuse him." She dabbed her eyes with a handkerchief.

But I was unrelenting. "All right, Mrs. Pumphrey, it's up to you, but I warn you that if you go on as you are doing, Tricki will go crackerdog more and more often."

I left the cosy haven with reluctance, pausing on the graveled drive to look back at Mrs. Pumphrey waving and Tricki, as always, standing against the window, his wide-mouthed face apparently in the middle of a hearty laugh.

But it was when the Christmas hamper arrived from Fortnum and Mason's that I decided that I was onto a really good thing which should be helped along a bit. Hitherto, I had merely rung up and thanked Mrs.

Pumphrey for the gifts, and she had been rather cool, pointing out that it was Tricki who had sent the things and he was the one who should be thanked.

With the arrival of the hamper it came to me, blindingly, that I had been guilty of a grave error of tactics. I set myself to compose a letter to Tricki. Avoiding [my partner] Siegfried's sardonic eye, I thanked my doggy nephew for his Christmas gifts and for all his generosity in the past. I expressed my sincere hopes that the festive fare had not upset his delicate digestion and suggested that if he did experience any discomfort he should have recourse to the black powder his uncle always prescribed. A vague feeling of professional shame was easily swamped by floating visions of kippers, tomatoes and hampers. I addressed the envelope to Master Tricki Pumphrey, Barlby Grange, and slipped it into the post-box with only a slight feeling of guilt.

On my next visit, Mrs. Pumphrey drew me to one side. "Mr. Herriot," she whispered, "Tricki adored your charming letter and he will keep it always, but he was very put out about one thing—you addressed it to Master Tricki and he does insist upon Mister. He was dreadfully affronted at first, quite beside himself, but when he saw it was from you he soon recovered his good temper. I can't think why he should have these little prejudices. Perhaps it is because he is an only dog—I do think an only dog develops more prejudices than one from a large family."

Entering Skeldale House was like returning to a colder world. Siegfried bumped into me in the passage. "Ah, who have we here? Why I do believe it's dear Uncle Herriot. And what have you been doing, Uncle? Slaving away at Barlby Grange, I expect. Poor fellow, you must be tired out. Do you really think it's worth it, working your fingers to the bone for another hamper?"

Even in the most high-powered small-animal practice with a wide spectrum of clients, Mrs. Pumphrey would have been remarkable, but to me, working daily with earthy farmers in rough conditions, she was almost unreal. Her drawing-room was a warm haven in my hard life and Tricki Woo was a loveable patient. The little Peke with his eccentric ailments has captured the affection of people all over the world, and I have received countless letters about him. He lived to a great age, flop-botting but happy to the end. Mrs. Pumphrey was eighty-eight when she died. She was one of the few who recognized herself in my books, and I know she appreciated the fun because when I stopped writing about her she wrote to me, saying, "There's nuffin' to larf at now." I wonder if she had her tongue in her cheek all the time?

Christmas Eve
from *101 Dalmatians*

DODIE SMITH

The Dalmatian army was swinging along the road in fine style. Though cold, the night was very still. The pups were rested and hopeful. And the fact that a tired little dog could take a rest with the Cadpig in her cart made tired little dogs feel less tired. Indeed, Missis at first had to insist that the smaller pups take turns to rest. But progress was not really fast. There were so many pauses while the pups who pulled the cart were changed, pauses while pups got in and out of the cart; and every half-mile the whole army had a rest. Still, all went wonderfully well until they were within half a mile of the village where they were to spend the day.

There was still a hint of dawn in the sky now, but

Pongo felt sure they could reach the village before it was dangerously light. He quickened the pace slightly and told the pups to think of breakfast ahead of them at the bakery.

It was soon after this that the Cadpig called out, "Look! Little painted houses on wheels."

Pongo saw them at the same moment, and he knew they were not houses. They were caravans.

He had seen them once when out with Mr. Dearly and had heard Mr. Dearly say that gypsies lived in caravans and gypsies sometimes stole valuable dogs.

"Halt!" said Pongo instantly.

Could they get past the caravans without being seen? He wasn't going to risk it. Between them and the nearest caravan was an open gate. He would lead the puppies through it and take them through the fields until they were well past the caravans. Swiftly he gave his instructions, which were handed on from pup to pup: "We are to keep dead quiet and follow Pongo through the gate."

And thus did the owner of one of the keenest brains in Dogdom make one of his few mistakes. For in the caravan nearest to them an old gypsy woman was awake and looking out of the little back window. She saw the approaching Dalmatians and at once woke her husband. He was beside her at the window just as Pongo led the way into the field.

The old gypsy woman never read newspapers, so she knew nothing about the stolen puppies. But she knew that here were many valuable dogs. And she knew something else, which Pongo did not know. There is a connection between Dalmatians and gypsies. Many people believe that it was the gypsies who first brought Dalmatians to England, long, long ago. And nothing like as long ago that, there were gypsies who traveled round England with Dalmatians trained to do tricks. And these performing dogs earned money for the gypsies. The old woman could remember such dogs, and she thought how splendid it would be if all these Dalmatians could be trained as money-earners.

"Quick! Close the gate!" she said to her husband. She spoke in the strange gypsy language, which is called Romany. "The only other way out of that field is through a break in the hedge. I will rouse the camp, and we will stop all the dogs there and catch them."

In less than two minutes the whole gypsy encampment was awake. Children cried, dogs barked, horses neighed. It was still so dark that it took Pongo five minutes to find the break in the hedge. And when he found it, he also found the way barred. All the gypsies were there, with sticks and ropes.

"Back to the gate, as fast as you can!" he cried to the pups.

But when they reached the gate it was closed. They were trapped.

Pongo barked loudly, hoping that some gypsy dog might help him. Many gypsy dogs barked in answer, but they had all been shut up in the caravans in case they should fight the Dalmatians. In any case, they barked only in Romany, so they could not understand a world Pongo said.

But someone else did. Suddenly Pongo heard the high neigh of a horse close at hand—and, oh, most wonderful, the horse could neigh normally, as well as in Romany. It understood Pongo, and he understood it. Horses are nearly always friendly to Dalmatians—perhaps because of those days when Dalmatians were trained to follow carriages. This horse was not old enough to remember such days, but he took an instant liking to Pongo, Missis, and all the pups. If these pleasant creatures wished to come out of the field, nothing could be easier. He strolled up, opened the gate with his long, strong teeth, and swung it back. Out poured the puppies.

"Lead them past the caravans as fast as you can!"

Pongo shouted to Missis, and waited to see the last pup out of the field.

"What a *very* large family you and your wife have," said the horse. "My wife and I have never made more than the one. Well, good luck to you."

He waved aside Pongo's thanks and then, being a very tidy horse, he carefully closed the gate again. So never did the gypsies—all waiting at the break in the hedge—know how their prisoners got away.

Helter-skelter along the road went Missis, the puppies, and, finally, Pongo. (The pups who drew the Cadpig's cart stuck faithfully to their task.) The shut-in Romany dogs heard them and shook the caravans in their efforts to get out. Volleys of furious barking came from the little windows.

"The caravans bark but the dogs move on," remarked Pongo when he felt they were out of danger.

A few minutes later they reached the village where they were to sleep. The Sheepdog's friend, a handsome Collie, was waiting there to welcome them.

"No talk until you're safely hidden," he said. "It's almost light."

Quickly, they followed him across the village green to

three old gabled houses. The baker's was in the middle, between the butcher's and the chimney-sweep's. The baker and the butcher and the sweep were all widowers and, as it was Sunday, had already gone to spend Christmas with their married daughters, which was just as well.

The baker's shop would not have been nearly big enough to house all the pups, but luckily there was a large bakehouse at the back. And soon every pup was safely in and enjoying a splendid sausage roll. Pongo and Missis chatted to the Collie while they ate. He shook his head worriedly when he heard about the gypsies.

"A narrow escape," he said. "The trouble is that Dalmatians are such noticeable dogs. Ninety-nine of you together are spectacular—though I mean it as a compliment. You'd be much safer if you were black."

"Like that nice little pup over there," said Missis.

"What pup?" The Collie looked across the bakehouse, then said sharply, "That pup doesn't belong in this village. Who are you, my lad? Where have you come from?"

The black pup did not answer. Instead, he came running to Missis and butted her in the stomach.

"Here, hold hard, young man!" said Missis. Then she gasped. "Goodness, it is! It isn't. It *is* Roly Poly!"

The fat puppy who was always getting into mischief had found his way into a shed at the back of the sweep's house and had a fight with a bag of soot.

"Mercy, you'll need some washing!" said his mother.

Then it was that one of the keenest brains in Dogdom had one of its brainiest waves.

"Roly Poly," said Pongo, "was there a lot of soot at the sweep's?"

"Bags and bags," said Roly Poly.

"Then we are *all* going to be black dogs," said Pongo.

"Your husband is a genius," said the Collie to Missis as he showed them all into the sweep's shed.

There was any amount of soot—waiting to have done with it whatever sweeps do with soot.

"Ten dogs forward at a time!" commanded Pongo. "Pups roll! Pups rub noses!"

In a very short time there were ninety-seven pitch-black pups.

"And now, my love," said Pongo to Missis. "Let *us* take a roll in the soot."

Frankly, Missis did not fancy it. She hated soiling her gleaming white hair and losing its smart contrast with her beautiful black spots. But when Pongo had helped her with the final touches he said: "Why, Missis, as a black dog, you're slimmer than ever. You're positively *svelte!*" and then she felt much better.

Then Pongo said, "How does soot suit me?"

"Suit soots you beautifully," said Missis, and all the pups roared with laughter at her mistake.

Then they all went back to the bakehouse and settled down to sleep. The Collie said he would call them as soon as it was dark. They would have only five miles to go to another bakery—but he felt they should get the journey over early as he had heard there might be snow.

"But there may be cars on the road until late, as it is Christmas Eve and Sunday," he told them. "So you must go by the fields. I shall escort you. Rest well now."

Poor Missis! When she awoke in the late afternoon and looked around her, she dissolved into sooty tears.

"I can't tell one pup from the other now that they're black," she moaned. But she soon found she could, though she could never have explained how she managed it.

Another meal had been organized, but it was not all that could have been wished, because the butcher had meanly locked up his shop.

"This clears the bakery out," said the Collie, carrying

in the last stale loaf. "But there will be a good supper waiting for you. And the journey oughtn't to take more than three or four hours." He then went off to see if there was any news coming in by the Twilight Barking.

After half an hour or so, Pongo began to feel anxious. It was quite dark now; they ought to be off. What was delaying the Collie?

"Listen!" said Missis suddenly.

Very, very faintly, they could hear the Collie barking. He was calling Pongo's name, again and again.

Pongo and Missis ran out of the bakehouse to the little yard at the back. Now they could hear the Collie more clearly. But he was obviously some way off. Pongo barked in answer to him. Then swiftly the Collie told them what had happened.

He was locked in a house across the green, with no hope of getting out. The postmistress had promised to look after him while the baker was away for Christmas. She had decided it was too cold a night for a dog to be out, hauled him in, and gone out for the evening. He had tried every door and every window but could undo none of them. It was impossible for him to escort the Dalmatians, as he had promised.

"But you *can't* miss your way, Pongo," he barked. "Out over the field at the back of the bakehouse and *straight* on for five miles."

Pongo told him not to worry. But the poor Collie was most unhappy. "Here I am, locked in with a warm fire and a good supper—and powerless to help you."

"And now, off we go," said Pongo, bringing the pups out of the bakehouse. "And no straggling! Because it would be very easy to lose a black pup on a dark night."

But it was not really a very dark night, for already the moon was rising and the stars were out. There was one specially large, bright star.

"The Collie said straight ahead, and that star is straight ahead," said Pongo. "So we'll steer by it." He was thankful they were going by way of the field and not by the road—for he remembered that Cruella had told the Baddun brothers she would come down "tomorrow night" to count the bodies. Now it *was* "tomorrow night" and the great zebra-striped car would be somewhere on the road from London to Suffolk. How terrible it would be to meet it! He imagined the glare from the headlights, imagined Cruella driving straight at the army of panic-stricken puppies. Yes, he would certainly avoid the roads! But, even so, it was frightening to know that

Cruella might be quite near. He put the thought from his mind as he and Missis got the pups into marching order.

Their way lay through grassy meadows over which the Cadpig's car trundled smoothly. At every hedge and ditch Pongo paused and counted the pups to see none had strayed, and Missis changed the pups who drew the cart and the pups who rested in it. Already even the smallest puppies were getting hardier—even the Cadpig got out of the cart and walked three fields before getting in again.

"Soon we shall be able to do ten miles a day," said Pongo.

They had traveled about three miles when the first disaster of the night happened. There was a sudden bump, and a wild squeal from the Cadpig. A wheel had come off the little blue cart.

Pongo saw at once that the cart could be mended. A wooden peg which fixed the hub of the wheel to the axle had come out. But could he ever, using his teeth, put this peg back? He tried—and failed.

"Could the Cadpig manage without the cart?" he whispered to Missis.

Missis shook her head. Walking three fields had been enough for her smallest daughter. And her other daughters could not walk more than a mile without a rest.

"Then mend the cart I must," said Pongo. "And you must help me, by holding the wheel in position."

They tried and tried, without success. Then, while they were resting for a moment, Missis noticed that many of the pups were shivering.

"They'd better keep warm by running races," said Pongo.

"But that would tire them," said Missis. "Couldn't they all go to that barn over there?"

They could see a big tiled roof, two short fields away— not very clearly, because the moon was behind the clouds; it was this lack of light which made it so hard to mend the cart.

"That's a good idea," said Pongo. "And when the cart's mended, we can bring it along and call for them all."

Missis said the Cadpig had better stay in the cart and keep warm in the hay, but the Cadpig wanted to go with the others and see the barn—she felt sure she could walk two short fields. So Missis let her go. Two strong pups the right size to draw the cart stayed behind. They said they did not mind the cold.

So ninety-five pups, led by Lieutenant Lucky, set off briskly for the barn. But when they got there it did not look at all like the barn at the Sheepdog's farm. It was built of grey stone and had long windows, some with coloured glass in them, and at one end was a tower.

"Why, there's a Folly!" said the Cadpig, remembering the tower of the Folly at Hell Hall.

Lucky was looking for a door, but when he found one it was firmly shut. He told the pups to wait for him while he went round the building looking for some other way in.

The Cadpig did not wait. "Come on," she said to her devoted brother Patch. "I want to look at that Folly."

And when they got to the tower they saw a narrow door that was not quite closed. It was too heavy for them to push, but they could—just—just—squeeze through.

Inside, this tower was nothing like the one at Hell Hall. And it opened into the grey stone building.

"No hay in this barn," said the Cadpig.

She had counted on the hay for warmth, but she soon found she was warm enough without it, for there was a big stove alight. It had a long iron pipe for the chimney, which went right up through the raftered ceiling. The moon was out again now, and its light was streaming in through the tall windows, so that the clear glass made silver patterns on the stone floor and the coloured glass made blue, gold, and rose patterns. The Cadpig patted one of the coloured patterns with a delicate paw.

"I love this barn," she said.

Patch said, "I don't think it *is* a barn." But he liked it as much as the Cadpig did.

They wandered around—and suddenly they made a discovery. Whatever this mysterious place was, it was certainly intended for puppies. For in front of every seat—and there were many seats—was a puppy-sized dog-bed, padded and most comfortable.

"Why, it's just *meant* for us all to sleep in!" said the Cadpig.

"I'll tell the other pups," said Patch, starting for the door. A glad cry from the Cadpig called him back.

"Look, look! Television!"

But it was not like the television at Hell Hall. It was much larger. And the figures on the screen did not move or speak. Indeed, it was not a screen. The figures were really there, on a low platform, humans and animals. Most lifelike, though smaller than in real life. They were in a stable, above which was one bright star.

"Look at the little humans, kneeling," said Patch.

"And there's a kind of cow," said the Cadpig, remembering the cows at the farm, who had given all the pups milk.

"And a kind of horse," said Patch, remembering the helpful horse who had let them all out of the field.

"No dogs," said the Cadpig. "What a pity! But I like it much better than ordinary television. Only I don't know why."

Then they heard Lucky and the others, who had found their way in. Soon every pup was lying curled up on a comfortable dog-bed and fast asleep—except the Cadpig. She had dragged along one of the dog-beds by its most convenient little carpet ear, and was sitting on it, wide awake, gazing and gazing at this new and far more beautiful television.

Once the moon came out from behind the clouds Pongo managed to mend the wheel—oh, the feeling of satisfaction when the peg slipped into place! Missis too felt proud. Had she not *held* the wheel? She, a dog who had never understood machinery! Quickly the two waiting pups seized the crossbar in their mouths. Then off they all went to the barn.

But as they drew nearer, Pongo could see that this was no barn.

"Surely they can't have gone in *there*?" he said to Missis.

"Why not, if they were cold?" said Missis. "And they are far too young to know they would not be welcome."

Pongo and Missis both knew that humans did not like dogs to go into buildings which had towers and tall, narrow windows. They had no idea why, and had at first been a little hurt when told firmly to wait outside. But Mrs. Dearly had once said, "We would love you to come in if it was allowed. And *I* would go in far more often if *you* could." So it was obviously one of those mysterious things such as no one—not even humans—ever being allowed to walk on certain parts of the grass in Regent Park.

"We must get them out quickly," said Pongo, "and go on with our journey."

They soon found the door in the tower—which the biggest pups had pushed wide open. Because Missis had always been left outside, she disliked these curious buildings with towers and high windows; but the minute she got inside she changed her mind. This was a wonderful place—so peaceful and, somehow, so welcoming.

"But where are the pups?" she said, peering all around.

She saw lots of black patches on the moonlit floor but had quite forgotten that all the pups were now black. Then she remembered and as she drew nearer to the sleeping pups, tears sprang to her eyes.

"Look, look at all the puppy-beds!" she cried. "What *good* people must live here!"

"It can't be the kind of place I thought it was," said Pongo. He was about to wake the puppies when Missis stopped him. "Let me sit by the stove for a little while," she said.

"Not too long, my dear," said Pongo.

He need not have worried. Missis sat still for only a few minutes. Then she got up, shook herself, and said brightly, "Let us start now. Things are going to be all right."

An hour or so later, just before the evening service, the Verger said to the Vicar, "I think there must be something wrong with the stove, sir."

On every hassock he had found a small circular patch of soot.

About the Authors

Teoti Anderson, Certified Pet Dog Trainer, is the owner of Pawsitive Results, LLC, in Lexington, South Carolina. The author of *Your Outta Control Puppy* and *The Super Simple Guide to Housetraining*, she serves as the president of the Association of Pet Dog Trainers. Teoti also volunteers as a Delta Society Pet Partner and teaches others how to visit patients with their pets.

Laurien Berenson has written twenty-four books, including romance and suspense. She is perhaps best known for her Melanie Travis dog cozy mystery series. Her books have appeared on the Waldenbooks bestsellers lists and won the Dog Writers Association of America's Maxwell Award for fiction four times. Her short story "Sleeping Dogs Lie" was nominated for Agatha and McCavity Awards. She lives in Kentucky, with her husband and their son.

George Berger is the publisher of AKC (American Kennel Club) magazines and books. His canine partner is

Dixie, a small yellow Labrador retriever who was originally trained to be a Seeing Eye guide. George and Dixie live in Battery Park City, Manhattan.

Mary Bloom has been a professional photographer specializing in animals since 1978. Her photographs have appeared in numerous publications, including *Life*, *Smithsonian*, *Woman's Day*, *Family Circle*, *People*, *The New York Times*, and the *New York Daily News*. She also has myriad book credits. Bloom has worked with the North Shore Animal League in Port Washington, New York, for twenty-five years, photographing shelter animals in need of homes.

Nancy Campbell has been breeding and showing performance shorthairs for nearly two decades. She is the chairperson of National German Shorthaired Pointer Rescue and has fostered more than 700 dogs through her home.

Judy Conner is a Renaissance woman. She is passionate about many things. Her prizewinning roses and camellias delight the visitors to her home, The Snuggery. She began reading her "Brown Dog Tales," the basis for her book *Southern Fried Divorce*, at the Sunday Salons in the French

Quarter of New Orleans, and several were featured in the Faulkner Society *Double Dealer*. She is the older sister of Jill Conner Browne, author of the bestselling *Sweet Potato Queen* series. Raised in Jackson, Mississippi, Conner now lives in New Orleans with her brown dog.

Amanda Craig was born in South Africa in 1959 and grew up in Italy. She was educated at Cambridge and is the author of five novels, the most recent being *Love in Idleness* (2003), published by Nan Talese at Doubleday. She is a columnist and critic for *The Times*, *The Sunday Times*, and *The New Statesman* (all in London). Her website is www.amandacraig.com.

James Herriot's bestselling series of memoirs includes *All Creatures Great and Small*, *All Things Bright and Beautiful*, *All Things Wise and Wonderful*, *The Lord God Made Them All*, and *Every Living Thing*. His veterinary practice in Yorkshire, England, is now tended by his son, Jim Wight.

Jon Katz has written twelve books—six novels and six works of nonfiction. A two-time finalist for the National Magazine Award, he has written for *The New York Times*, *The Wall Street Journal*, *Rolling Stone*, and *Wired*. He is a contributing editor to National Public Radio's *Marketplace* and to *Bark* magazine. A member of the Association of Pet Dog trainers, he lives in northern New Jersey with his wife and daughter and their two dogs.

Trish King is the director of the Animal Behavior and Training Department at the Marin Humane Society in Marin County, California. She wrote the dog training manual, *DogSense* and *Parenting Your Dog*. Trish has a formerly stray, anxious German shepherd, one sweet female Belgian Tervuren, one challenging rescued Cairn terrier, one husband, and one teenage daughter.

Marion S. Lane cowrote *The Humane Society of the United States Complete Guide to Dog Care* and is the author of *The Yorkshire Terrier*, as well as almost one hundred articles about dogs. From 1986 to 1990 she was executive editor of *Pure-Bred Dogs/American Kennel Club Gazette*, the monthly magazine published by the American Kennel Club. She is currently an editor of special projects at the American Society for the Prevention of Cruelty to Animals in New York City.

Matthew Margolis began his dog training career in 1968 and established the National Institute of Dog Training, which became one of the largest dog training facilities in the United States. In addition to the series *Woof! It's a Dog's Life!*, his expertise and winning personality are well known to television viewers throughout the United States, Canada, and parts of Europe. Margolis was the resident dog expert on ABC's *Good Morning America* and continues to be a popular guest of news and talk shows. He has appeared on ABC's *20/20*, *The Oprah Winfrey Show*, CNN, and E! Entertainment Television, among others. Margolis is the coauthor of seventeen books on dog training and behavior. Visit www.unclematty.com for more information.

Susan Chernak McElroy is the author of *Animals as Teachers and Healers*, *Animals as Guides for the Soul*, and *Heart in the Wild*. She offers lectures and workshops worldwide and lives in Idaho.

Emma Mellon grew up in southwest Philadelphia. She graduated from Temple University, moved to Washington, D.C., to teach language arts in a private school, and then returned to Temple and earned a Ph.D. She is a licensed psychologist in private practice and an author of nonfiction and poetry. Her work has been published in *The Philadelphia Inquirer* and the Philadelphia *Daily News*.

Willie Morris wrote *North Toward Home*, *New York Days*, and two novels. As the imaginative and creative editor of *Harper's*, he was a major influence in changing our postwar literary and journalistic history.

Susan Orlean is the *New York Time*–bestselling author of *The Orchid Thief*, *The Bullfighter Checks Her Makeup*, and *Saturday Night*. She has been a staff writer at *The New Yorker* since 1992. Her articles have also appeared in *Outside*, *Rolling Stone*, *Vogue*, and *Esquire*. She lives in New York City with her husband, John Gillespie. For more information on her, visit www.susanorlean.com.

Colleen Paige is a dog trainer, animal behaviorist, author, TV personality, and founder of National Dog Day. She lives in Seattle with her husband, son, and a menagerie of critters big and small. Visit her on the Web at www.colleenpaige.com, www.nationaldogday.com, or www.universitydog.com.

Liz Palika has been involved with purebred dog rescue for almost thirty years, working with German shepherd, Australian shepherd, and papillon rescue. An award-winning author and professional dog trainer, Palika specializes in training rescue dogs and their owners to enable these dogs to remain forever in their new homes. The bimonthly columnist on purebred rescue for the *AKC Gazette*, Palika has written over fifteen books.

Michael Paterniti is the author of the bestselling book *Driving Mr. Albert: A Trip Across America with Einstein's Brain*, which first appeared as an article in *Harper's*, winning a National Magazine Award. He is a frequent contributor to NPR's *This American Life* and has written for various publications, including The *New York Times Magazine*, *Esquire*, *Outside*, *Rolling Stone*, and *GQ*, where he is an editor-at-large.

George Rodrigue was born in New Iberia, Louisiana, in 1946. Artistically trained in California and New York, he became well-known for his distinct, primitive images of Cajun subjects, and especially for his creation of the ubiquitous "Blue Dog." Among his most famous works are *The Ailloli Dinner* and *Three Oaks*. He has exhibited his work at major galleries in the United States and abroad. Rodrigue owns a Lafayette restaurant called Cafe Tee George.

Shel Silverstein was best known for his nine children's books, which have sold over 18 million copies in hardcover and have been translated into twenty different languages. A true Renaissance man, Silverstein wrote Johnny Cash's number-one hit "A Boy Named Sue," as well as several plays, including the 1981 hit *The Lady or the Tiger Show* and *Remember Crazy Zelda*? He collaborated with David Mamet on the play *Oh, Hell!* and the 1988 film *Things Change*. In 1984, he won a Grammy for his recorded poetry collection, *Where the Sidewalk Ends*.

Dodie Smith was born Dorothy Gladys Smith in Lancashire, England, on May 3, 1896. Smith's autobiography was published in four volumes: *Look Back with Love: A Manchester Childhood; Look Back with Mixed Feelings; Look Back with Astonishment*; and *Look Back with Gratitude*. Probably best known for her novel *101 Dalmatians*, Smith wrote numerous books for adults and children as well as several plays. She died in 1990.

Steve Swanbeck started writing about abandoned and abused animals in the early 1980s during his days as a newspaper editor and helped many unwanted dogs and cats find new homes. He has more than twenty years' experience writing professionally and is the author of *Disposable Dogs*, *East Hanover*, and *The Seeing Eye*.

Three Dog Bakery was started by **Dan Dye** and **Mark Beckloff** in 1989 with a rolling pin, a wooden bowl, and a 59¢ biscuit cutter—and their dogged determination to create the world's best dog biscuit ever! From their bare-bones beginnings, they are now opening dozens of Three Dog Bakeries nationwide and have built wholesale and mail-order divisions. They have become known nationally through their televised cooking show *Three Dog Bakery ... Unleashed!*, viewed and enjoyed by dogs throughout the U.S.A. on the TV Food Network. Call 1-800-4TREATS for a free DOGalog, or sniff around the website at www.threedog.com.

Connie Wilson is creator and publisher of *Modern Dog* magazine. Inspired by the growing dog culture and her love for her dog Kaya, she dreamed up a glossy publication that would be reflective of the urban dog lover's lifestyle. With

Connie at the helm, *Modern Dog* has become *the* magazine of choice for dog lovers the world over. Celebrities—from Pamela Anderson to Virginia Madsen to Paris Hilton—and their dogs have graced the cover, and Kaya herself has "penned" articles and starred in photo shoots. To check out Connie's vision, visit www.moderndogmagazine.com.

Credits and Permissions